Also by M. A. Bennett

*Young Gothic*
*Children of the Night*
*No Escape*

# A DEADLY PLEDGE

## M. A. BENNETT

WELBECK
CHILDREN'S BOOKS

WELBECK CHILDREN'S BOOKS

First published in Great Britain in 2026 by Welbeck Children's Books,
an imprint of Hachette Children's Group

1 3 5 7 9 10 8 6 4 2

Text copyright © M. A. Bennett, 2026

The moral right of the author has been asserted.

*All characters and events in this publication, other than those clearly
in the public domain, are fictitious and any resemblance to
real persons, living or dead, is purely coincidental.*

All rights reserved.
No part of this publication may be reproduced, stored in
a retrieval system, or transmitted, in any form or by any means, without
the prior permission in writing of the publisher, nor be otherwise circulated
in any form of binding or cover other than that in which it is published
and without a similar condition including this condition being
imposed on the subsequent purchaser.

A CIP catalogue record for this book
is available from the British Library.

ISBN 978 1 804 53623 0

Printed and bound in Great Britain by Clays Ltd, Elcograf S.p.A.

The paper and board used in this book
are made from wood from responsible sources.

Welbeck Children's Books
An imprint of
Hachette Children's Group
Part of Hodder & Stoughton Limited
Carmelite House
50 Victoria Embankment
London EC4Y 0DZ

The authorised representative in the EEA is Hachette Ireland,
8 Castlecourt Centre, Dublin 15, D15 XTP3, Ireland (email: info@hbgi.ie)

An Hachette UK Company
www.hachette.co.uk

www.hachettechildrens.co.uk

To my friendly neighbourhood flock of pigeons
for their feathery inspiration

Content warning: strong language, alcohol consumption, violence, death and dead bodies

# PROLOGUE

Bartholomew Van Buren III knows exactly the moment that he's going to die.

Forcing himself to stay calm, he assesses the situation:

He is trapped underground, in a seven-by-two-foot coffin, the air stifling, oxygen rapidly running out. Added to that, his mortal enemy is standing on the lid, so he cannot escape.

But even now, that indomitable little flame called Hope burns stubbornly and will not be extinguished. Surely this is part of the pledge? Surely his enemy will relent, open the lid and pull him to freedom? Surely they will all laugh about this later, about how scared he had been?

But then he hears the voice he knows as well as his own, from six feet above. And the sound that tells him it is over:

The brutal death rattle of earth hitting the coffin lid.

# PART 1

## The Count of Monte Cristo

'All human wisdom is contained in these two words; Wait and Hope.'
*The Count of Monte Cristo* – Alexandre Dumas, 1846

There's something rotten in the state of Connecticut.

By way of an example, let me tell you what happened to me tonight.

So, I'm working as a cater-waiter at this bougie upscale school in Washington, Connecticut, the little town where the tide washed me up. I'm just clearing the plates after the dessert course (*dessert* course – can you believe that?) when this girl gets up from her chair and slaps me in the face.

She just straight up slaps me in the face.

I didn't spill meringue on her, or roll my eyes at her, or even nudge her chair. But suddenly she's on her feet, fronting up to me, my cheek is stinging and she's glaring at me with tears in her eyes.

Actual tears.

'Oh, so you are alive then?'

There's no real answer to this, so I shrug and say, 'Evidently.'

This just riles her up more. 'What are you doing here, pretending to be a regular Joe? One of the little people?' She narrows her pale-blue eyes at me. 'Oh. Is this another one of your little initiation challenges? Are you pledging again?'

My head is reeling, and not just from the slap. 'I don't . . . What do you . . . I mean . . .'

'Run out of words, have you?' The girl is really pretty and really blonde, and she's wearing this rose-pink silk ball gown. People would probably stare at her even if she wasn't screaming at me. But they are all looking now – all those privileged high school girls in their bright gowns, the faculty, the other waiters. She ignores them all.

'Well, you had plenty to say to me last fall when you fed me all that bullshit about my eyes being like stars, and that we were meant to be together and that it was written in the constellations.' A look of realisation crosses her face. 'Wait, was all that stars stuff because you knew I went to Ida Barney?'

'What's an Ida Barney?'

'Don't be funny. And what about New Year's at Yale Art Gallery? What about meeting under *Hero and Leander*? Did you think it was funny to leave me waiting there?'

'What the hell are you talking about?'

'And I can't believe you didn't even come back for the funeral. That was really low.'

Before I could ask what funeral, and for whom, Miguel, who has always been – and continues to be – an asshole, grips my upper arm hard enough to hurt and hauls me off to the kitchen. Amid all the steam and the yelling chefs and the percussion of the pans he tears the bow tie from my neck like he's stripping me of the purple heart.

'I knew you were a no-good sonofabitch as soon as I laid eyes on you,' he spits. 'Too much attitude, like you're someone. But you're no one. You're not fit to lick the boots of these young ladies. What did you do to that one? Pinch her butt?'

'No,' I say. '*No.*'

'Anyway. Get out of my sight.'

'Wait. What about my wages? I've worked this whole shift, nearly.'

'Don't make me laugh,' he snarls. '*¡Vamos!*' He shoves me towards the swing doors and I almost lose my balance. Miguel says he used to wrestle in Mexico. That's probably bullshit like everything else he says, but I'm not going to risk a beating. I shrug and turn on my heel.

The night is mercifully cool. The sky is clear and the stars are out. I look at the building, all lit up for the high school formal. It's more like a palace than a place of learning, and the windows watch me like eyes.

'Look all you want,' I say. I'll be damned if some entitled little snoot and a fake wrestler are going to throw me off the school grounds before I'm good and ready to go. I would have a really long leisurely smoke, then I would grind the butt of my cigarette into the manicured lawn. Or throw it in the silvery fountain. Whatever. Just a small rebellious action – a blot on the landscape, a fly in the ointment, a dead bee in the honeypot. That's me.

I sit myself down on the bowl of the fountain, and the stone is cold under my butt. In the centre of the sculpture a marble angel is spewing water, vomiting continuously like some of those high school girls inside will be doing tonight, judging by the amount they'd been obviously illegally pre-drinking. The night is dark blue, and black bats swoop and dive, shrieking as they slice the sky. I can hear the female voices inside, shrieking too. But out here it's cool, and quieter, and I am alone. Just how I like it.

I take my time, and after a long final drag I put the cigarette out on the sole of my rented shoe. But I don't throw the butt on the ground, nor in the gently splashing fountain. I tuck it neatly into my pocket. It's been a strange and horrible night. And I don't want to be part of the rottenness. I want things to be good and true again.

I'm about to get up, and head back to my rented room. Then I see a shape running across the lawn, blonde hair flying like a pennant, silk dress rustling. It's her. The girl who slapped me.

She comes up to me and sits down beside me, in a flurry and a bustle of silk, and puts a hand on my arm. The hand is warm and I'm cold. This is the second time she's laid an unwarranted hand on me tonight, but this time I don't really mind. It's better than the slap.

'Thank God you're still here. I'm so, *so* sorry. I asked your boss about you. He said your name is Ed.'

'Eddie,' I say. 'Eddie Dontay.'

'I thought you were someone else. I screwed up. I'm sorry. I'll talk to him – get him to give you your job back.'

I note the confidence of the rich. This princess has no doubt in her voice – no doubt at all at the age of what? Seventeen? – that she can talk to a middle-aged catering manager and get my job back. 'Don't bother,' I say. 'This is just an occasional gig. I got another job.'

'You have *two* jobs?' There it is again. That entitlement, oblivious to the notion that some jobs might be so poorly paid that you might have to have two just to get by. I imagine being like that.

'Yes,' I say. 'I work in Marty's Café in Washington. I'll be OK.'
'If you're sure?'
'Sure I'm sure. I wouldn't work for Miguel again if you paid me. Which is more than he did.'
'Of course.' She scrabbles on her shoulder for a strap and swings a little bag off her shoulder. It's the kind of bag that girls have that's not big enough for anything more than a cell phone and lip gloss. And cash. In this case, lots and lots of cash. She gets out a wedge of fifties and waves them at me. 'Is this enough?'

Another rich girl flex. Money makes everything go away. I look down at the bills, clasped in the hand that slapped me. It was more than enough; it was way too much. I would have had to work five high school formals to get that amount. But some nameless instinct, from another world and another life, makes me refuse.

'I don't want your money.'

She recoils, like she was the one who was slapped. She tucks the money away hurriedly. 'How clumsy. I'm making things worse and worse. I didn't mean to insult you.'

'You didn't insult me. But the slap I could have done without.'

She puts her head in her hands and groans. But then she takes it out again and looks at me. She's been looking at me intently throughout this whole exchange, as if she can't believe I'm real.

'Your hair is longer and lighter,' she says wonderingly, as if to herself. 'And he didn't have this scar.' She lifts her fingers to the scar above my brow, but this time she doesn't touch. I could tell her how I got it but she'd never believe me. 'But really it is incredible. Almost unbelievable. You look *just* like him.'

It's time to ask. 'Like who?'

'Bartholomew Van Buren III.'

The name, like a long-forgotten echo, rings in my head. It is a name from another world. A world where people have three names when one will do. A world where people have three generations worth calling the same thing.

'Who is . . . Bartholomew von Burns?' I take care to get the name wrong.

'Bartholomew Van Buren. It's a bit of a mouthful, isn't it? Everybody called him Brat.'

'Brat?' It occurs to me I should ask why. 'Why?'

'He used to act out at grade school. The other kids called him Brat and the name stuck.'

'How did you know him? And why are you so angry at him?'

She's silent for a moment, looking down at her rose-polished nails.

'You wanted to pay me. This is how you pay me. Quid pro quo for the slap.'

That was a mistake, speaking Latin, but she doesn't seem to notice. She shivers. It's pretty cold for a fall evening, and I seem to have a recollection of movies where the guy gives the girl his jacket. But I'm in white waiter's shirtsleeves so I've got nothing to offer her. And I'm not a hundred per cent sure I would give her my jacket even if I had one, since she slapped my face and got me fired. 'OK,' she says. 'Quid pro quo. I was seeing Brat. He goes – went – to New Haven, the boy's school at the other side of town. Do you know it?'

'No,' I say, a bit too quickly.

'We were . . . dating. And it seemed to be going really well.'

'So I gathered. All that stuff he said about the stars.'

She looks kind of embarrassed. 'Yeah. Now, of course I know it was a line. Like I said, he was using the whole constellations metaphor because he knew I went here. To Ida Barney.'

'Oh, so this is Ida Barney?' I say. 'This school?'

'Yes. Didn't they tell you when you got the job?'

'They just text you a zip code and time. There might have been a name, but I just thought that was the contact.'

'No. This is Ida Barney, the most prestigious girls' high school on the eastern seaboard.' There's pride in her voice. 'Named for Ida Barney, the female astrologer. Our school motto is *Ad Astra*. To the stars,' she explains, a little apologetically. I guess you can't expect a cater-waiter to know Latin. Maybe she's forgotten I've used it already. 'I'm also the editor of the student body newspaper, which is called *The Star*. Of course, Brat knew that. So the stars thing was all a line.'

She looks at me. Her eyes *are* kinda like stars. You can't see the blue in the moonlight, but they are as bright as mirrors. 'It might not have been a line.'

'It was,' she says. 'We arranged to meet at Yale Art Gallery just before midnight on New Year's Eve. Under a painting we both liked – *Hero and Leander* by Paul Rubens.' She doesn't ask me if I know it – waiters wouldn't.

'How would you get in there at midnight?'

'There was a benefit, for a charity – my mom's on the board.'

Of course. Normal opening hours don't apply to the rich.

'Anyway, he didn't turn up. I waited hours – right up until they closed the place. I stared at that painting for three straight hours. I know every brushstroke. I could make you a copy.' She's trying to make a joke of it, but you can tell she's still hurting. I feel sorry for her for the first time.

'What did you say when you called him?'

'He didn't pick up. No texts, no nothing. I asked some of his friends at his school. They said he took a sabbatical to go travelling. There's nothing on his socials, but Brat was never big on social media anyway. Some of his buddies got postcards from around the world, but I got nothing. He just . . . disappeared with no explanation. That's why I said *so you are alive then*.'

I nod, but there's one more thing to ask. 'Why did you ask if I was "pledging again"? If the whole waiter thing was an "initiation ceremony"?'

She goes quiet again, and starts picking a frill of lichen off the stone fountain with a pink fingernail. It's as if she's deciding how much to tell me. 'Because when I met him, he was in the process of pledging for a secret society. A very . . . *odd* secret society. Not one of your usual Greek letter, keg-sucking college fraternities. This one is different.' She looks back at me with her starlike eyes. 'It's called The Gloomth.'

How can a word pass through you like a knife, robbing you of breath? I compose myself before I speak again. Why would Eddie Dontay fear this word? Answer: he wouldn't. It's just a collection of letters, that together make a funny sound. 'The Gloomth?'

'Yeah. G-L-O-O-M-T-H,' she spells out. 'That's almost all I know. He didn't even want to tell me that much. The word just . . . slipped out, and then he looked horrified. Like he wasn't supposed to tell me. And there's another thing. I got to know him at the beginning of the fall term. Right about now, a year ago, a few weeks after the Ida Barney Commencement Dinner, which is what we had tonight. He was confident, funny, talkative. Looking forward to being a Squab – that's what they call the newbies in The Gloomth; apparently squabs are baby pigeons. By the last time I saw Brat he was . . . different.'

I'm interested. 'Different how?'

She wrinkles her nose like a bunny as she thinks. It's kinda cute. 'He was thinner. He had violet shadows under his eyes, like a vampire. And he seemed edgy, afraid. If I had to choose a word for it, I would say he looked . . . haunted.'

I shiver, and not entirely because of the cold.

'He would disappear for days on end. And then when I saw him again, he would have odd marks on him. Not wounds exactly, but a bruise here, or a rope burn. Or a strange smell around him. None of it was explained. All I knew is that he was pledging for this society, and that his initiation process took the whole of the first term, ending at Christmas break. I got the sense that all the challenges, whatever they were, were ramping up to the ultimate one – the biggie, right at the end of term. But after Christmas break I never saw him again.'

'You mentioned a funeral,' I say carefully. 'A funeral he didn't come back for. Whose was that?'

'Brat's great-aunt,' she says. 'She was like the princess of New England. Eye-wateringly wealthy, but nothing so vulgar as new money. The Van Burens had money, but also heritage, going right back to the founding fathers. She died in January.'

My insides do this weird thing, like when you go down in an elevator.

'Everyone thought that Brat would be bound to come back for the funeral, but he didn't. My family knew his slightly. It was a huge society funeral. Everybody went. Even me. Although to be brutally frank, I went to see if Brat would be there.'

Her honesty is disarming.

'I think . . .' she pauses. 'I think whatever he saw – or did – with The Gloomth, scared him so much that he had to leave and not come back, put as much mileage between him and that school as possible. Even to the point of missing his great-aunt's funeral.'

I think carefully before framing my next question. 'But what could be so bad that he would just quit like that?'

'That's just it. I don't know. I did the whole baby journalist thing, and tried to investigate, but I couldn't find anything online. No one in the school will talk about it, none of his friends; they just close up like Maryland clams. And I get the feeling they know. All of them. So that just left me with that one word: Gloomth. So I tried Google.'

'And?'

'Gloomth seems to mean the love of all things Gothic – associated with a cult of melancholy. Apparently the word first appeared in the 1700s in a letter written by Horace Walpole, an English author who was known as "The Father of Gothic".'

'Huh.'

'And that points to The Gloomth being some sort of literary society. But how would that be scary? I mean, *Oh no, I read Frankenstein and now I have to run away*?' She waves both hands and mimes in terror.

'I'm sorry,' I say. 'I've no idea. But I hope you find him.'

'Me too,' she says. 'I feel like we really could have had something. You know?'

The syntax of the question makes it sound like she's talking about me. 'Yes,' I say.

She straightens up, sniffs and smiles at me brightly. The tears standing in her starlike eyes make them shine even more. She slaps both hands to her thighs with decision, jumps up and holds out her hand. I automatically get up too, and after I figure out what's expected of me, I shake her hand.

'Good luck, Eddie Dontay. And *I'm* sorry. Again. About the slap.'

As she walks away it occurs to me that there is a question that I should have asked, but didn't. 'Wait! You never told me your name.'

She turns like Cinderella at midnight, her rose gown whirling around her.

'It's Harper. Harper Larsson.'

All I have to do is wait.

And hope.

And it works.

The girl who slapped me – Harper Larsson – is in the café again.

This is the third time now in one week, and it's no coincidence. Before the commencement dinner I'd never seen her here. Admittedly I haven't worked at Marty's for very long, but I definitely would have remembered seeing her.

I haven't been going out of my way *not* to serve her, but the first two times it was the breakfast shift and that's always pretty busy. Washington is this cute little town, with a clapboard church and a town square, and at the moment the chestnut trees are turning all the colours of fire. So, as well as the usual crowd – college freshmen, Yale students and hipsters who are writing the next Great American Novel on their typewriters – the place is full of leaf-peeping tourists. So both breakfast times I could do nothing more than glance over at Harper as I ran around serving waffles and pancakes and eggs over easy.

And every time I looked, she was looking at me.

This time, we are at the dog end of the evening shift. The last lingering customers are eking out their final latte of the day, conscious that there will be no more caffeine until morning if they want to get their eight hours. Stacey, who is the manager (Marty, whoever he is or was, is long since departed or deceased), is cashing up the till. Counting other people's money. She talks about buying the place one day but she'll never have the money. Just another working stiff, like me. Now there's nothing left for me to do but wipe down the tables. And now, finally, there's no avoiding Harper.

'Hi,' she says.

'Hi,' I say back. 'What a coincidence.'

'Not really,' she says. 'I'm stalking you.'

There's that refreshing honesty again.

'Can you sit? I'll buy you a coffee.'

I glance over at Stacey. 'Not really. I'm working. But I get off in five.'

Stacey smiles over at me in this motherly way. She's big and Black, beautiful inside and out, and she's always been kind to me. She swallowed my story – orphaned, a ward of state, found a job through the Connecticut outreach programme – and has always kept a lookout for me. She's heard everything, which is not surprising. The place isn't large and we are the only people in here apart from a couple of guys with sleeve tattoos and man buns. Stacey's always worried about me having no friends or family, so the fact that this cute girl seems to be hitting on me has made her day. At least she's a decent human, unlike Miguel.

'Go on, honey,' she says. 'Take a load off. I'll finish up here.'

'Thanks,' I say gratefully, and slide into the booth opposite Harper. Outside it's already dark, since we are in September, but the street lights are warm and the bandstand has fairy lights. It's all super romantic, and to anyone looking in on this Edward Hopper painting it would seem like we are on a date. But I know Harper's not here for romance. My spidey senses know she has another motive entirely.

Stacey comes over with two cups of coffee then goes back to the till. Harper leans in, bright eyes fixed on me. 'I have a business proposition for you.'

So it begins. Half of me is disappointed, but my heart begins to speed, just as if she *had* actually asked me on a date. 'Go on.'

'I want you' – she looks at her coffee as she stirs it rhythmically, creating a little vortex – 'to go to New Haven School, as Brat, and re-pledge for The Gloomth.'

She's created a whirlwind in me too. 'What?'

'Something is going on there,' she says. 'Something rotten.'

I'm reminded of what I thought that night at Ida Barney. Something rotten in the state of Connecticut. 'But I have a job. How am I going to earn money?'

'This is a paid gig.'

'Who is going to pay me?'

'I am,' she says simply.

'I wouldn't take a few dollars from you the other night. What makes you think I'll take a wage?'

'I came into a trust last year when I was sixteen. Another matures next year when I'm eighteen. Then a third when I'm twenty-one.'

I reflect again on the safety, the comfort of wealth. Like a warm coat.

'Why would I take this job?'

'Because you need it. And because you're a good person.'

'How do you know?'

'Because you are the kind of person who tucks a cigarette butt in his pocket, rather than litter a green lawn. Yes. I saw.' She lifts her eyes from the coffee to me. And I do feel seen. Having Harper think of me as a good person is addictive. 'I think if you can find out what is happening at The Gloomth, you will make the world a better place. Remember, Brat had all the wealth and privilege in the world, and something traumatised him so much that he ran away. What if some scholarship kid comes to New Haven, or some newbie from outside the area, and gets himself killed?'

I think about this. She makes a good point. A good person, if that is what I am, would do anything to prevent some other kid suffering. But I still have my doubts. 'No one would buy it for a single second. There are too many traps. There will be his friends, the teachers; they will all know him from before.'

'Not well. He only had a term there – he transferred for his junior year. And as for all the society kids you're going to meet' – I note she's talking about it like I've already agreed – 'I will train you. I've been steeped in Connecticut society since I was born. The Larssons were some of the original Swedish immigrants to Delaware. We've been in the country almost as long as the Van Burens. And they practically came over on the *Mayflower*.'

I say nothing for a moment, just looking at her, marvelling again at the sheer confidence of the very rich.

'Eddie,' she says. She covers my hands with hers, and out of the corner of my eye I see Stacey smirking triumphantly. 'I can't *tell* you how much you look like him. With a haircut, and the school uniform, you'll be his absolute twin. You've even got the eyes. Those curious Van Buren eyes. You can see them in portraits. Amber, like a fox. You *must* be a relative, somewhere down the line.'

'Maybe,' I concede cautiously. 'My mom used to say we had family round these parts. Maybe that's what drew me here.'

'There you go.' She shrugs.

'What about ID?'

She spreads her hands. 'What ID? You're not enrolling. You're just returning to your school. All that paperwork will already have been done.'

'And fees? A place like New Haven isn't exactly going to be free.'

'Again. Your' – she catches herself – '*Brat's* lawyers will already have paid the fees for last year. But Brat was only there for one semester. You won't owe anything until Easter.'

'There's one last thing you haven't thought of. What if the *real* Brat Van Buren turns up?'

She shakes her head. 'School started this week. That's why we had the commencement dinner. New Haven keep the same dates as Ida Barney. If he's not enrolled yet for this year, he's not going to. At least, not this semester. And you only need one semester to figure this thing out. Like I said, all the pledging is done by Christmas. It ends with the big challenge – whatever that is – just before the holidays. And there's another thing. If you do this, you'll have a whole team behind you.'

'How's that?'

'You'll have my team. I'm the editor of *The Star*, remember – Ida Barney's student newspaper? You've got a whole squad of baby Woodwards and Bernsteins salivating at the scent of a good story. They've got more connections than the National Grid, and they all want extra credit for their Ivy League applications. We can get hold of records, research, data, recording equipment. Satnav, trackers. You'd be totally supported. And if we crack this Gloomth thing wide open, we're talking Pulitzer material.'

'Calm down, Scoop,' I say. 'It's way too dangerous. You've got nothing to lose, except money, and you've got plenty of that. I could go to jail.'

'You're a minor. They don't jail people until twenty-one.'

'Juvi then.'

'Then I'll sign a contract with you. A document of liability. I'll take all the blame. You'd just be a contractor.'

It's time for the bait and switch. 'I'm sorry. The answer is no.'

She doesn't try to convince me, but gets to her feet. 'Look. Just think about it. That's all I ask.'

Of course, I do think about it. I think about it as I help Stacey close up. I think about it while I'm batting away her questions about the 'nice young lady'. I think about it on the walk home. Which always takes me a while because I take a circuitous route in case of being followed.

When I get in, I look at myself in the dingy square of mirror in the corner of my room. When I look in it I am transformed into one of those portraits that Harper referenced. I regard myself as if I'm looking at a stranger, someone brand new. I see what she means about the eyes. Amber like a fox. Or amber like a hare. Predator or prey, which one am I? Then I think about a different metaphor. Amber preserves things. Amber oozes from primordial trees, traps insects in its sticky heart for millennia. The amber Van Buren eyes, watching the centuries roll by since the ink dried on the constitution. Keeping everything the same, guarding their wealth like a greedy dragon, as a new country became an old one. The Van Burens, a rich family getting richer, with no one to challenge their place in society, their age-old entitlement. Well, that's about to change.

I'm going to do it.

Actually I have known I was going to do it all along.

Harper comes back the next morning, just as a good reporter would. I knew she'd be here. Today she's in her uniform – a distinctive bottle green with yellow piping. It suits her, but then everything seems to suit her. She looks like one of those girls they put in the prospectus to lure people to the school. She sits at the window table, and this time I serve her right away. 'Hi, Scoop,' I say. Tomorrow is Saturday and we make an arrangement to meet at the Yale Art Gallery.

'There will be quite a crowd, and we'll just disappear,' she says.

'OK,' I say. 'Where will I find you?'

'Under *Hero and Leander*, of course.'

'You're gonna have to help me out here,' I say.

'Sorry.' She smiles goofily and shakes her head. It's adorable. 'I keep forgetting you're not him.' She scribbles a schematic on a napkin. 'Sackler Wing, second floor, Renaissance Art.'

I wait until after the breakfast rush to help Stacey out, then when the last customer has gone I quit my job. Stacey looks genuinely sorry, and gives me a warm hug. It's the first human contact I've had in forever. Beside the slap, of course. I'm genuinely touched.

'You found somethin' else?' she asks. 'None of my beeswax, of course.'

'Yeah. I got another job.'

She nods. 'You're a good kid,' she says. 'But it's a tough old world out there. You gotta do what them pigeons do. Shit on everyone else before they shit on you.'

I smile. Stacey always says that. 'I will.'

I open the door and the little brass bell above it starts ringing. It's a clarion call, a starting pistol.

'Come back and see me, ya hear?' she calls after me.

I turn. 'I will,' I promise. 'I won't forget you, Stace.'

On the way out I dump Harper's napkin map in the trash.

I'm not gonna need it.

The next day I'm at Yale Art Gallery before it even opens. It's a beautiful building, more like a church than a gallery, with a four-square tower, arched windows and a cloister of golden stone. It looks gorgeous surrounded by the autumn trees; the maple and the birch and the ash are the hues of a forest fire. I have to get used to walking into beautiful buildings as if I belong there. I find my way to *Hero and Leander* with no trouble at all. Surefooted, unaided, through galleries painted in primrose, teal, duck egg; expensive colours as a backdrop for priceless art. I'm deliberately early because I want to know what it's like to wait by that painting. I need to know what it felt like for Harper that New Year's night, waiting for Brat.

The painting, hanging on a coffee-coloured wall, is fabulous.

No wonder it was Brat's favourite. I look at it like I once looked at my reflection, as if for the first time.

It's a masterpiece. It depicts a boiling black lake, with naked twisted bodies breaking the surface like sea foam. A knife strike of light slicing through the morbid clouds illuminates the broken body of a man, grey and lifeless, held aloft by nymphs. A woman on the shore cries inconsolably. My eyes focus on the man, his flesh lacerated by rocks and weed, a poor drowned wretch. And suddenly something happens to me. I can't catch my breath. The gallery disappears and I'm far down in the jade-green water, choked by weeds, tugged by currents, drowning. I gasp, throat tightening, sweat springing to my skin. I'm sinking, sinking, way out of my depth.

'Do you like it?' Harper is at my shoulder.

I snap back to the present. 'I think it's amazing.' I turn to look at her. She's in casual gear, but she still manages to look expensive. The jumper she's wearing screams cashmere, and the ski jacket is a brand that would cost two months of my pay packet from Marty's.

'It illustrates the ancient Greek legend of Leander, who swam a treacherous stretch of water called the Hellespont in order to meet with Hero, his lady love. One dark and stormy night he perished in the waves, and Hero threw herself into the water to join him in death,' she says, by way of greeting.

'Cheerful,' I say. 'Do you know why Brat chose this painting specifically? As a meeting place, I mean? It's hardly a story for a date night.'

'No,' she says. 'I guess he just liked it.'

So there are some things she *doesn't* know.

'Let's take a walk,' she says.

We do. And for the rest of the morning, strolling those rarefied galleries, observed by the snooty portraits of New England's great and good, she begins to school me in everything I will need to know.

Yale Art Gallery was just the beginning. We meet every day, before or after school, always a different place, so if this all goes to shit we won't have been seen plotting. Cafés mostly, galleries sometimes. Harper's methods are simple. She gives me this huge information dump, which I have to memorise, then drills me relentlessly on what I've learned. She shows me resources that exist already – like the New Haven prospectus – which I then have to memorise, but she doesn't create a study pack for me or anything like that. The napkin that I dumped in the trash is the only thing she's ever written to me, and she's very strict that I can't write anything down either.

'No notes,' she says. 'No crib sheets, no jotters. It's for your own protection. We can't have any evidence that this is a sting.'

Harper would fire questions at me like bullets:

'Can you name the tombs in the New Haven chapel from left to right?'

'What animal is featured in the stained glass of the library window?'

'What are the names of the four school houses?'

'Get me from the dormitory to the refectory. Go via the principal's office.' She throws this at me when we're walking across Criscuolo Park, and the dog walkers and frisbee throwers are treated to the sight of a tall guy, blindfolded by his companion's scarf, weaving his way across the leaf-strewn grass.

While Harper is at school, I spend my time studying too. I haven't done any book learning for a while – on the state's outreach programme I chose to work, not go to high school. But Harper gets me a pass to the Washington Library, and I spend hours reading up on the history of Connecticut in general and the Van Burens in particular.

Even to the initiated, it's an impressive story. If the Van Burens didn't actually come over on the *Mayflower* they were pretty damn close. Dutch settlers who founded the New Netherlands, the Van Burens were among the first to purchase a packet of land on Manhattan in 1631. A few short generations later, Martin Van Buren was in the White House, the only president in history not to have a British background, and who spoke English as a second language. It seemed odd to me that he was once an outsider, this founding father. I'm impressed.

I meet Harper at the Washington Square bandstand with the confidence of someone who knows the Van Burens inside out. She wastes no time. 'You went to a wedding of the Coney Island Van Burens in the summer of 2024. Who was getting married?'

'Mr Cornelis Maessen Van Buren and Miss Halley-Rose Winslow of the Long Island Winslows. Father of the bride Richard, mother Emily.'

She nods once. 'Bunny Van Buren had the same nightcap every night for fifty years before retiring to bed. What was it?'

I don't even have to think about this one. 'Whiskey and tepid water, with a teaspoon of powdered ginger.'

'Trace me the Van Buren family tree from President Martin Van Buren to your paternal grandfather.'

'Martin Van Buren Junior, Winfield Scott Van Buren, John Vanderpoel Van Buren, Smith Thompson Van Buren, Bartholomew

Van Buren I,' I rattle off, allowing myself a cocky smile, 'who was my grandfather.'

She looks at me sharply. 'Good,' she says grudgingly.

We talk a bit about how plausibly late I could be for the beginning of term, and we conclude that after more than a couple of weeks they might give away Brat's school place, since New Haven, according to Harper, is hugely oversubscribed and sharp-elbowed parents will do most anything to get their precious sons in.

My gut feeling is that during all this disclosure she is keeping something back, just as I am. You can always recognise your own traits in another, like looking in a mirror. There is something unspoken, something difficult and dangerous, something that could be a wrecking ball to the whole enterprise. And so it proves. The Something finally comes up when we are in our millionth café, this one by the harbour in Grape Vine Point. There is an unusual darkness in her light eyes as she pushes her coffee away. Harper exhales a long breath and says, 'It's time to tell you about the Parslows.'

I look out at the little boats tacking on the water, and the little clapboard harbour houses with their red roofs, while I frame my next question. In the end I opt for simplicity.

'Who are the Parslows?'

She fixes me with her blue eyes. 'The Parslows are the rival family to the Van Burens. You've heard of the Jets and the Sharks, the Montagues and the Capulets, the Hatfields and the McCoys? Well, the Van Burens and the Parslows are worse. They've been sworn enemies for hundreds of years.'

'How did it start?'

'Some land dispute on Manhattan Island in the seventeenth century. The origins are so unclear now that no one can really remember how it began. But what we *do* know is that it carried on for centuries. In the Gold Rush one Floyd Parslow stole Randolph Van Buren's gold, and Randolph Van Buren shot Floyd Parslow's mule. The Parslows and the Van Burens were on opposite sides of the Civil War. Then there was a duel over a woman, between Tolbert Parslow and Ellison Van Buren, and Ellison Van Buren got shot. And so on and so forth, right up to the present day.'

'And who do I have to worry about now?' I ask. 'Who's the current Parslow MVP?'

She hesitates for a moment. 'Ulysses. Ulysses Parslow.'

The name gives me a feeling like when you're going down in an elevator.

'And what do we know about him?'

'Ulysses Parslow is in his last year at New Haven, and is the current president of The Gloomth.'

'But what do we *know* about him?'

'Quite a lot, actually. You see' – she lets out a breath, or is it a sigh? – 'we grew up together.'

'You *grew up* together?' I repeat.

'In a manner of speaking. Our families were close, and we used to summer in Nantucket together. We'd spend Christmas together too, until . . .' She tails off.

'Until?' I prompt.

'There was this one Christmas at the Parslow house in Rhode Island. We were fourteen. There was a big freeze that year. We used to skate on the lake every day. His sister . . . His sister fell through the ice. She died.'

'That's awful,' I say, meaning it. 'No, that's really awful. And awful for him. Life changing.'

'Yes. I mean . . . Yes, it is. Obviously. But I never saw him shed a tear. All that Christmas. I'd seen him way more upset than that. Years before. Over something much less significant.'

Now she looks out at the boats.

'We were in Nantucket. There was a little island off the shore and we used to take this little rowing boat out to it. All us kids – my kid brother Stellan, Ulysses and his sister Timmie.'

'Wait,' I say. 'This kid is called Ulysses and they called his sister something super plain like Timmie?'

'No,' says Harper. 'She was christened Ctimene. In Greek mythology Ctimene was the younger sister of Ulysses. Well, Odysseus, but you know what I mean.'

I did.

'One time we saw this duck stuck in a fishing net. A really cute duck, beautiful plumage, all green shot with blue, eyes like black beads. It was twisting and twisting, and of course the more it twisted, the more it got stuck. We all rowed over there to try to help. We reached out with the oar, to try to pull the net off, but it had got one of its wings tangled and was listing, like a shipwreck. It kept rolling under the water then up again – over and up, over and up.' She swallows. 'He was in a bad way. Ulysses and I waded in. I reached out to untangle it – and this I'll never forget. He stopped me. He held my arm, hard enough to hurt, and held me back. He stood there, knee deep in the warm tide, and watched the duck die.' She fixes me with her gaze. 'He just watched it die.'

'Wow,' I say. 'I've heard of little boys pulling the legs off spiders but that's next level.'

She nods. 'It was like he was one of the old gods, wielding the power of life and death. There was no compassion, no pity. Just a fascination.'

'Jeez,' I say. 'That's cold.'

'Yes. But then, that night, he started crying about the duck and just couldn't stop. He was inconsolable.'

'Maybe he felt guilty.'

'Yes. But there was something more than that. He just – gave into it. Let the tide wash over him. Like he was *enjoying* the grief. Then two years later when Timmie went through the ice, it was the same again. All through the terrible bits while his mother and father were dealing with the EMTs and the hospital, then the police and the DA's office and the press, he was stoic and composed. But at the funeral – *boy*.'

'Bad?' I ask.

'Never seen anything like it. A tsunami of tears. He howled in that church like a wolf. It was chilling.'

'Understandable though,' I say, striving to be fair. 'I mean, his little sister had just died.'

'Of course. But it just felt a little bit . . .'

'A little bit . . . ?' I prompt.

'I don't know,' she says. 'Self-indulgent.'

I absorb this. 'And are you still friends?'

She lifts one shoulder and drops it again, an asymmetric shrug. '*Kind* of. Our families are still close. But like I say, he's not the Ulysses I used to know.' She wrinkles her brow, trying to articulate what she's thinking. 'He's such a contradiction. He must be one of the most beautiful humans on the planet.' I feel a jag of jealousy. 'But he has an ugly soul. He's empathetic but also a psychopath. He's utterly charming but can be cold and dismissive. He was a complicated little boy and now he's a complicated young man.'

I look at my grimy, bitten nails. 'Do you think he had something to do with Brat leaving?'

'No, not that,' she says. 'Their families have been at daggers drawn since the birth of this nation. But Ulysses Parslow was only pledging too last year, just like Brat. I don't think he had anything to do with Brat running away. The blame for that lies elsewhere. With someone far more powerful.'

'When am I gonna find out about *him*?' I ask.

Harper studies me. 'We have to do something about the way you speak.'

It's such an abrupt change of direction that she wrongfoots me. 'What's wrong with the way I speak?'

'Gonna,' she says. 'Wanna. Coulda, woulda, shoulda. It all has to go. You have to have the clipped, New England society speak. We'll practise as we go. You could start by copying me.' She smiles. 'And once you're in New Haven you'll have the best elocution tutors in the world – the Gothic Boys. You can just copy them.'

'Who are the Gothic Boys?'

'The members of The Gloomth, of course. That's what they call themselves. The upper cohort left last year. That leaves four remaining members, and they'll be looking for three more. There's our friend Ulysses Parslow, he's the leader. Then there's Ignatio Jorquera, also known as Iggy. He's Spanish royalty on his father's side, I believe. Very confident, lots of flair and charm. Then there's Oliver Arblaster – he's of English ancestry. Thin, bespectacled, almost transparent. His family actually *did* come over on the *Mayflower*. Then there's Lowell Bell-Cross. A solid New England family heir, an ace rower, very WASPy and athletic. Lowell's the opposite of the type you'd expect to be devoted to Gothic literature. But he's just as evangelical about it as the rest of them. And they're all on the Committee of Taste, a little ruling party who decide on the society's dress codes, and the furniture and pictures for their common room, and everything they eat and drink. Because there is a social side to their society. Dinners, parties, gatherings. They are very exclusive. The main one is the Feathers Ball and it's coming up in a couple of weeks. That's quite open – all the New Haven seniors go as well as The Gloomth, and all the Ida Barney seniors. And it's held at New Haven. I suppose even The Gloomth feel like they need some social skills around women, if they are going to make good marriages and have little Gothic Boys of their own.'

'Why the "Feathers" Ball?' I ask.

'Not sure,' she says. 'I can only assume it's something to do with the pigeon connection, which I still don't fully understand.'

I did, but I say nothing.

'And everyone has to wear feathers – that's the dress code.'

'You mean like . . . feather boas?' I ask.

She laughs – it's a nice sound. 'No. It's not *RuPaul's Drag Race*. Just there must be a feather element to what you wear. Last time I wore a feather headband. Brat asked me to the ball, almost exactly a year ago.' Suddenly she's someplace else, thinking about the boy who's gone. And once again I am fiercely jealous, which is ridiculous.

'The other person you need to know about, the most important piece on the chessboard, is Lewis Walpole.'

I know my lines by now. 'Who is Lewis Walpole?'

'He's the literature professor at New Haven. He's knee-deep in The Gloomth.'

'You mean he's a member?' I ask carefully.

'No, not that exactly. But I think the whole thing was his idea. It's one of the oldest societies at New Haven, and he's one of the oldest members of staff, if not *the* oldest. I think he founded it. He was at the school, years ago, then he went to Oxford in the UK, and as soon as he graduated he was back here teaching. He must have been there fifty years.'

I give a long, low whistle. 'That's quite a shift.'

'Yup. The other thing to know about Lewis Walpole is that he has this fabulous Gothic reproduction villa in the Connecticut Hills. That's where he reportedly spends weekends and vacations.'

'He's pretty rich then?' I ask, my voice loaded with a suitable amount of envy.

'Hell, yes,' she says. 'Extremely wealthy.'

'So why does he bust his ass teaching high school lit?' I ask.

'He loves it,' she says simply. 'He *lives* for Gothic literature. Gothic is his birthright, if you think about it. His villa is supposed to be an exact reproduction of Strawberry Hill House in England, the family seat of Lewis's ancestor Horace Walpole.'

'What was his deal?' I ask.

'Remember? I told you on the night of the Commencement Dinner.'

I duck my head. Sometimes it's hard to remember what I'm supposed to know and what I'm not supposed to know.

'It's OK,' she says. 'I know it's a lot to take in. You've been bombarded with facts for a fortnight. Horace Walpole invented the word *Gloomth*. And wrote the first ever Gothic novel. He was an English politician and writer, living in the eighteenth century. He wanted to build himself a Gothic palace in the English countryside, a haven for everything in the Gothic aesthetic, and he formed a Committee of Taste to consult with his highfalutin friends on what should be in there. That's where The Gloomth got the idea for their committee. Quite an elitist idea if you think about it. Telling everyone else what they should like, being the arbiter of good taste.'

'Kind of like the first influencers,' I say.

'Exactly that,' she says. 'Anyway, Horace Walpole is the touchstone for this whole thing.'

'You say he wrote the first Gothic novel?' I say. 'What was it?' Because you would ask, wouldn't you?

'Tomorrow.' She looks at the setting sun, drowning in its own blood over the harbour. 'I have to get back before curfew.'

# PART 2

## The Castle of Otranto

'A bystander often sees more of the game than those that play.'
   *The Castle of Otranto* – Horace Walpole, 1764

The next day I'm in the Washington Library as soon as it opens. I'm the first one there. Harper is the second. She's in her uniform again, because of course she will be going straight to class. As she gets closer, I can see that the breast pocket of her blazer has a crest featuring one yellow star. She marches over to my table and thumps a book down in front of me.

'This is the Bible.'

I look at the book. It's not *the* Bible. But it could be. It looks pretty old and is bound in black leather so ancient it looks almost green. On the cover, in faded gold relief, are the words THE CASTLE OF OTRANTO BY HORACE WALPOLE. It lies there in a pool of light, all the hues of the stained glass of the windows of the library, but still manages to look like a vacuum, an absence, a void. Something with a strange power, a darkness about it.

'Enjoy,' says Harper brightly. 'I'll see you at lunch.'

'Where?' I ask.

'At the café, of course,' she says. 'Where else?' And she disappears, leaving her smile behind, like the Cheshire Cat. But even that, and the lingering memory of her bright beauty, isn't enough to keep at bay the cold feeling of foreboding that seems to have set up camp in my stomach. I really, really don't want to open the book.

I'm afraid.

Then I give myself a good talking to. I know there's nothing to be afraid of, nothing between these pages anyway. So I open the cover and start to read.

As ever, once buried in a book I am lost to the world. The bells of the church ring the hours four times unheeded, I successfully ignore a bothersome bluebottle butting at the stained glass, but the rumbling of my stomach won't be disregarded, and intruding thoughts of lunch make me shut the book. I've always been a quick study so I've almost finished, and as I sit at a table in the café, demolishing a Reuben on rye as I wait for Harper, I reflect on what I've read. When she arrives she orders a coffee and gets straight down to it.

'So,' she says, 'what's it about?'

I think for a moment. 'The Castle of Otranto tells the tragic history of its lord, Manfred, and his family. It begins on the wedding day of Manfred's son and heir Conrad, who is crushed to death when – and go with me here – the giant helmet of the statue of a knight falls on him before he gets a chance to say "I do". Manfred fears that an ancient prophecy about his family is coming true – that "that the castle and lordship of Otranto should pass from the present family, whenever the real owner should be grown too large to inhabit it." Manfred decides to marry Conrad's bride, Isabella, and divorce his own wife, Hippolita.

'Isabella escapes her fate with the help of a peasant called Theodore, who helps her take sanctuary in the church. The church's friar refuses to let Manfred violate sanctuary to get his bride-to-be back. Theodore is revealed to be the friar's long-lost son, identified by a mark on his shoulder, and therefore of noble birth. Isabella hides in the labyrinthine crypts of the church, and Manfred suspects Theodore is meeting her there for secret trysts. He sneaks in and stabs a woman he thinks is Isabella, but is actually his own daughter, Matilda. Effectively his line of Otranto is ended, and an apparition declares the prophecy has come true and shatters the castle walls. Theodore becomes Lord of Otranto, marries Isabella and presides over the ruins. Do I have it right?'

'Pretty much,' she says. 'And what did you think of it?'

I shrug. 'I dunno.'

'*I don't know*,' she corrects. 'Try to articulate what you feel. This is exactly the kind of thing you'll be asked in class with Professor Walpole. And you have to be on your game. So let's practise.'

'Well,' I begin, 'it is an oddity. If it had come at the end of a long line of Gothic novels you might think it a parody. Mistaken identity, a long-lost heir, the death of the head of the house, a giant ominous statue, a castle, a beautiful imprisoned heroine, a weak ineffectual nobleman, a brave stranger. But this book came at the start. It was the beginning.'

'Good,' she says. And coming from her, that single syllable means a lot. 'And it's helpful that you've read the whole thing. Because when you pledge for The Gloomth, the first thing you have to do is recite a passage from it from memory.'

'Oh, come on!' I plead. 'There's no way anyone could memorise the whole thing.'

'Obviously,' she says. 'They tell you which passage. But you have to get it *exactly* right. And they get you to drink while you're doing it. And every time you get so much as a word wrong, you have to take a shot.'

I swallow, as though I'm downing one right now. 'How do you know all this?'

'Brat had started the process before the Feathers Ball. I got the impression he was sort of boasting – trying to impress me. It was quite sweet. Of course, he told me about the first pledge before he knew he wasn't supposed to. And at the ball he was wearing The Gloomth uniform, so I know about that. It's a black suit with a tailcoat and a white cravat.' Her face changes. 'It was the last time I saw him happy. Before he became afraid and closed up like an oyster.' She gives herself a little shake. 'Anyway, that's about the only thing I know about the pledges. When Brat was worrying about what he'd have to do, I asked him why he just didn't ask one of the boys in the year above. He told me that would be futile because a) the first rule of The Gloomth is you don't talk about The Gloomth, and b) the other pledges change every year.'

'And that's everything you know?'

'Almost,' she says. 'That and the fact that all the pledges to follow are based on Gothic literature. So you'd better do some prep.'

From that day in the Washington Library, my reading changes. I'm no longer reading the family trees of the Van Burens and the Parslows. I immerse myself in Gothic books, poems, novellas. It seems that Ida Barney has a good literature programme too, because Harper is able to help me with most every text. We form our own book club, and in the endless rotating cafés we discuss everything I've read, from modern classics like *The*

*Bloody Chamber* back to actual classics like *Frankenstein*. These sessions are illuminating and I learn a lot from her, but the only thing she can't tell me, the only passageway in this maze of knowledge that remains terrifyingly dark, is anything else to do with The Gloomth. Of that she knows nothing but the very sparse details that Bartholomew Van Buren III had told her before he got drawn into the darkness, been pledged and terrified and changed. The Walpole link, *The Castle of Otranto*, the baffling connection with pigeons.

Harper is all business. There is nothing of the affection she must have formerly felt for Brat, to wait for him for all those hours by *Hero and Leander*. There is no trace of the passion, the hurt that she'd displayed when we met, the night of the slap. I continue, in a teasing way, to call her 'Scoop', so focused is she on getting the big story. We are a business arrangement, a shared goal, nothing more. And as if to put the seal on that, we sign a contract. She brings a sheaf of papers with her to the next café, a pleasing little place in New Milford. She turns the pages round in front of me, unscrews the cap of her fountain pen (of course) and places that on top of the document.

I pick up the pen and scan the contract, my skin prickling with sweat. I had hoped she'd forgotten about this. I'm going to have to do some fast thinking.

Next to NAME I write *Eddie Dontay*.

'Full name, please,' she says at once.

'How do you mean?' I act stupid, vamping for time.

'Eddie is a contraction. You need to write Edward. Or Edgar, like Poe.'

'Edmond, actually.'

'OK. Edmond. Now address.'

'Number 34 Wilmore.' I write it down.

'How about a character reference? A personal referee.'

'I got no one.'

'*I haven't got anybody*,' she corrects me. 'Just someone who can prove you are who you say you are.'

'There's Stacey at Marty's Café,' I say.

'How long has she known you?'

'About three months.'

'How about before that?'

'OK, well, there was a priest at the mission. Abbot Faria.'

'He'll do,' says Harper. 'Write him down. Have you got a contact number for him?'

'No. They don't let you have their personal details when you're a ward of the state. But you can get him through the pro bono lawyers of the family court,' I say.

'OK. Write them down as a contact,' she says. I duly write *Thompson & French, Attorneys-at-Law*.

I have to be careful about how I write my Ss. Habit is a prison.

'Now sign.'

I haven't really got a signature, so I just write E-D-M-O-N-D D-O-N-T-A-Y.

'That reminds me,' she says, watching me write. 'We have to get you to forge Brat's signature.'

I have a feeling that would be easier than what I had just done.

For the final week the preparation becomes even more relentless. We go back over everything we have learned and Harper makes it her business to catch me out. Only once I best her. We're in a Washington café poring over *The Abridged History of New England* (an ideal sedative if you ever have trouble sleeping) and she finds a Van Buren family tree.

'What was Bitsy Van Buren's maiden name?' she asks, covering the page with her hand like I'm trying to copy her homework.

Not for the first time I reflect on the absurd nicknames of the rich. Bitsy, Bunny. Bitsy Van Buren was an obscure cousin twice removed, but I answer straight away. 'Gilmore.'

'Close,' she says. 'It was Gilchrist.' Then she uncovers the book and checks. 'Oh no. It *was* Gilmore. My bad.'

I do a little mime like I'm brushing something off my shoulders, as it seems like the thing to do when you get one up on somebody. But it's a warning. I'll have to be careful.

'OK,' she says, sitting back in her chair and regarding me through narrowed blue eyes. 'I think you're ready to meet the team.'

'What team?' I ask.

She drains her latte before answering. 'The crack journalists and ace reporters of the Ida Barney *Star*,' she says 'Remember?'

It's the second time I've been to Ida Barney in work clothes, and this time I am just as invisible as the last.

Harper had stolen me the overalls and baseball cap of a janitor. They are sludge green with the golden star crest of Ida Barney on the breast pocket, and they make me disappear as surely as a cloak of invisibility. It's the lunch hour when I walk into the school uninvited, and despite the establishment being chock-full of the Daughters of the American Revolution, no one challenges me. The passageways are probably busier than they would be when school is in session, with various scary-looking female teachers swooping along the corridors like bats in their academic gowns, but none of them glance beneath the peak of my cap. Once again I reflect on the difference between Eddie Dontay and Brat Van Buren.

I am well used, by now, to memorising routes in buildings I'm not supposed to be in. So I find my way sure-footedly to the press room of the student newspaper. Lesser schools would make do with an empty classroom or school library for the student newspaper to operate, but not Ida Barney. The room I enter could have been the press room of the *Washington Post*, with the latest tech cluttering desks, a dozen reporters hunched over laptops and various layouts and mock-ups and digital photos stuck to a state-of-the-art magnetic brainstorm board.

Everyone looks up when I enter the room. Everyone but Harper looks back down. The camouflage of the uniform again.

Harper jumps up to greet me.

'Hi, Scoop,' I say.

She doesn't answer directly but drags me to the centre of the room. 'Ladies,' she says to the collective, 'meet the story.'

It's odd being introduced in that way – to stand in the middle of that press room, to take off my hat (as a gentleman always should in the presence of ladies) and go from invisible to being the laser focus of a dozen pair of eyes in an instant.

'Eddie, meet the team.'

Someone kicks a wheeled office chair towards us at speed. Harper stops it with her foot, turns it round and pulls it over to a desk with three girls sitting around it. 'Take a seat,' she says. She herself perches on the edge of the desk like one of those casual news anchors, and when I try to give her the seat she refuses. There's no doubt who is in charge. 'Eddie,' she says, 'meet Stevie, Reuter and Anna Sato. This is the core team who will be working on your undercover exposé.'

'Hey,' I say with a little head-bob.

'Or,' says Harper sternly, '*I'm delighted to make your acquaintance, ladies.*'

I bow more formally. 'Delighted to make your acquaintance, ladies.'

I look at the three girls. Their uniform is the same but the resemblance ends there. The first has a short crop and a lively, intelligent face. The second has a lot of unruly red hair and a sprinkling of freckles beneath her glasses. And the third has a black sheet of hair and a serious expression. I look back at the second girl. 'Your name is Reuter?'

'It's Rita,' she says. 'But since I joined *The Star* everybody calls me Reuter. Because of the press agency, you know.' I do know. But I pretend I don't.

'OK,' says Harper. 'Enough chit-chat. Let's get on with it. Anna Sato is our resident Chinese tech support. She's got your new phone.'

Anna passes me a brand-new iPhone, the latest spec, which I suppose Brat would have.

'New Haven don't allow phones during the school day,' Anna says. 'And even in the dormitories you're only allowed them for one hour of recreation time in the evening. *But* you can use them at weekends, and it's good to have one for emergencies, just in case some serious shit goes down.' I search her face for signs of a joke, but she is completely deadpan.

'Reuter is our art department,' continues Harper. 'Photography, layouts and all of that visual stuff.'

'I found a family photo online from your cousin Artie Van Buren's eighteenth birthday,' says Reuter. 'I've cleaned it up and airdropped it to your cell. If you open it up it should be on your camera roll.'

I handle the phone. It is cool and sleek and heavy, and feels expensive in my hand. 'What's the code?'

'Your birthday,' says Anna. 'You remember when it is, right?'

I do indeed. I tap in 170808 and the phone unlocks.

'If you could navigate to photos, and make it your wallpaper, that makes it seem convincing if someone should happen to pick it up,' says Reuter.

There's only one photo in the camera roll. So odd to begin again, to have such a blank canvas, a life with no memories in it. I set the photo as my wallpaper and am lost for a minute gazing at Brat Van Buren. He is smiling, looking directly at the camera, with the amber Van Buren eyes. He has his arms thrown casually round two other young fellows who have the family resemblance stamped on their faces. All three are clearly Van Burens, all are dressed in white tie and tails, but I only have eyes for Brat. What must it be like to have that life? I guess I'm going to find out. I notice that they all have a small gold pendant hanging beneath their ties. 'What's with the necklaces?' I ask.

'That's the Van Buren medallion,' says Anna. 'Every Van Buren boy gets one at the age of sixteen. We've got one for you.'

She reaches into her desk drawer and brings out a little thread of sunshine. She dangles the medallion in front of my face like she's trying to hypnotise me. When the pendant stills I can make out the design – a shield featuring two medieval-looking houses side by side. Just looking at it gives me a funny feeling. 'As you probably remember from your study, the name Van Buren means "neighbour" in Dutch,' says Harper. 'Hence the two houses.'

I look at the design. To me, now, it doesn't mean friendliness and amity. It means two households, both alike in majesty, at daggers drawn. It had been Harper who had said Montagues and Capulets. I am about to start the latest battle in a centuries-old war.

'This one isn't actually real gold,' adds Anna, 'so don't try to sell it on Craigslist.' Again, I search her face for a joke: nothing. 'It's a reproduction. But it has one very special feature.' She breaks the thing open with her thumbnail and I see it has a little hinge, like a locket. Inside, instead of a curl of hair like in all the Gothic novels I've been reading, is a tiny cluster of electric components – a mini motherboard and an LED light. 'It's a GPS tracker,' she says. 'That way we know where you are at all times.'

I put the medallion on and centre it over my heart. It's cold initially but heats immediately, and it warms me to know that it's there. At least I won't be alone. 'What if they steal it? The Gloomth?'

'My guess is they will leave it on you,' says Anna. 'Ulysses Parslow will want to beat a Van Buren. If your identity is taken from you there's no victory for him.'

Harper looks at her sharply. I get the feeling she is defensive about her former friend.

'Well,' I say. 'It will be good to have some surveillance.'

'You'll have more than just the GPS if things go to plan,' says Harper. 'When I was at the Feathers Ball with Brat he was wearing another piece of jewellery, even more distinctive than the Van Buren medallion.'

'What was it?'

'Stevie?' Harper makes a gesture, handing over to the girl with the short crop and the turned-up collars. 'Stevie's our resident hacker.'

Stevie sits back down at her monitor and deftly taps a few keys. A black and white video springs to life on screen, playing in a loop. 'This is CCTV from the Feathers Ball last year,' she says. I peer at the screen. Two people are walking through a doorway, under a banner that says BIRDS OF A FEATHER FLOCK TOGETHER. One of the people is Harper, in a column dress and a feather headband.

The other person is me. Or someone who looks identical to me. Brat.

He's wearing a black suit, a white cravat and what looks like a feather thrust into his pocket instead of a handkerchief. It's so odd to see your image like that – yourself and yet not yourself. I look at the young man in the footage as intently as I looked at the young man in the picture on the phone.

'Now look more closely,' says Stevie. She punches into the freeze-frame, zeroing in on Brat's neck. The image becomes more pixelated and granulated, but I can just make out the tie pin at my twin's throat. It looks like the head of a bird. No: the *skull* of a bird.

'What is it?' I ask.

'That,' says Harper, 'is the tie pin they give you when you're pledging The Gloomth. It shows that you're in the process of initiation. Apparently it's life size – solid silver cast on the skull of an actual pigeon. It's the first thing I remarked on when Brat asked me to dance. And here's the crucial thing he told me. When you're pledging, you wear it upside down, with the beak pointing to the left. The French word for left is *gauche*,' she explains, clearly for my benefit, 'and in English gauche means clumsy or unfinished. Brat told me that when you are accepted into The Gloomth proper you're permitted to turn the pin around and wear it with the beak facing right. I started noticing that night, and sure enough, all the Gothic Boys had their skulls the right way round.'

'So is that what you meant by surveillance?' I ask. 'You're going to hack into the CCTV?'

'I might,' says Stevie, like it's nothing. 'But I actually meant we are planning to plant a camera on you.'

'How?' I ask.

Anna takes over. 'In the skull,' she says. 'It's ideal. According to Brat you have to wear it at all pledges. It has a cavity, as all skulls do, and an eye hole for the lens.'

'Is there a camera that small?' I wonder aloud.

Anna snorts. '*Is there a camera that small*,' she repeats scornfully. 'Of course.' She goes to her drawer again and rummages around. She opens her fist under my nose and something small sits on her palm, no bigger than one AirPod. 'It's Sprite 3000,' she explains. 'The same camera used in drone technology. It's wireless and connected to my laptop. We just need the housing and you're going to take care of that.'

'Of course, you'll have a day or two without us, before the first pledge,' says Harper.

'Assuming they *invite* me to pledge,' I say. 'Again.'

'They will,' says Harper, as surely as I've ever heard her say anything. 'You are unfinished business. And then, at the Feathers Ball, which is Saturday week, Anna will bring the camera. All you have to do is ask her to dance.'

'It would be my pleasure,' I say with the olde worlde courtesy Harper has taught me.

'Can't wait,' Anna says drily, and I start to really like her.

'You said a couple of days without you,' I say. 'That means . . .'

'Yes,' says Harper. 'You start Monday.'

I swallow. That's in three days. For a second, abject terror washes over me, and I feel as if I might fall over.

If Harper notices, she says nothing.

'Stevie hacked the offices of Theodore Seamark, the Van Buren lawyer, and got a template for his headed notepaper rerouted to our printer. We sent a letter to the Principal of New Haven School to tell him that you would be returning next week. All you have to do is keep your cool and remember everything you've learned. We're going to bust The Gloomth right open.' She lays a reassuring hand on my arm. 'This is going to be the scoop of the century.'

The bell sounds for the end of lunch. That's my cue to go. I stand. 'Thanks, everyone,' I say. 'I guess I'll see you around.'

'You certainly will,' Harper says. 'This weekend we are all taking you for your glow-up.'

That last weekend before starting school, Harper, Anna, Reuter and Stevie take me to various august establishments around the area, studiously avoiding New Haven. Harper says that since Brat was a well-known ladies man it wouldn't be unusual to see him with a bunch of different girls, but that she and I should get out of the habit of being seen together exclusively.

I reflect on how different that is to my real self – I've felt like any confidence I might have once had with women was well and truly dead and buried. But I obediently let the quartet of reporters take me to the school outfitters, the barbers, the shoemakers and the tanning salon. This last is Harper's idea.

'You've been travelling for a year,' she explains. 'You've got to look like it.' We concoct a story based on the postcards the Gothic Boys have reported receiving – the Maldives, Maui, Dubai. Harper pronounces me to be finally ready and, as a final test, we decide we'll go back to Marty's on the very Monday morning I am due to start at New Haven. Stacey is the only person who had really known Eddie Dontay, and if she doesn't recognise me, I might be in with a shot.

When I walk in, it is the breakfast rush, but instead of being a waiter I am now a customer. I've gone up in the world. I choose a booth in back and Stacey barely looks up from her notebook when she serves me. I order a coffee in my new clipped accent, and she clearly doesn't recognise me. Paradoxically, I have mixed feelings about that. Part of me is relieved – I've passed the test. Part of me wants to junk the whole thing, confess to her and sob into her bosom. But she bustles away to get my order, and the moment passes.

I gaze at myself in the mirrored wall of the diner while I wait for Harper. I don't blame Stacey for not knowing me. I am transformed.

My bleach-blond surfer hair is gone, and I have a preppy crop of brown curls. Luckily, I had about two inches of roots, so the barber didn't have to do any dyeing at all, he just had to shear me of my golden fleece. I also had a shave with a Sweeney Todd-style razor.

'This could hardly be more Gothic,' I remarked to Anna, who had accompanied me. Anna didn't smile. She never did. Now, in the mirrored wall I observe my clean-shaven self. Stubble gone, I simultaneously look younger and also older than I did. Something about the shave and the haircut has given my face new angles, and thanks to the tanning salon I have a golden glow which makes my fox eyes – Van Buren eyes – sing out. I'm wearing the New Haven uniform, an achingly well-cut suit of black with red piping on the blazer and a black and red tie. In the mirror I can't see the Van Buren medallion, but I feel its reassuring metallic warmth beneath the collar of my crisp white shirt and it's good to know it's there. It feels like the one item that completes this disguise – this identity I have claimed:

Harper arrives and orders a latte. We go over all the New Haven stuff one more time. Staff, geography, customs. The Gloomth. The Gothic Boys. Ulysses Parslow. And the mysterious professor, Lewis Walpole. At the end of it all she takes a breath.

'Are you ready?' she asks.

'I don't know,' I say.

'I think you are,' she says, smiling. 'A few days ago you would have said *dunno*. Remember, as soon as you get the pigeon skull, let us know. And before I forget.' She passes a sheaf of notes across the table. 'Petty cash.'

I look at the money. I wouldn't take it before, but now I'm on the payroll. 'Thanks,' I say. I take all of it, except a fifty-dollar bill that I leave for Stace. I look apologetically at Harper. After all, it is her money. But she looks unconcerned.

'Actually, that's a very Brat thing to do,' she says. 'He was very open-handed with his money. It was nice of him.' Suddenly she's far away again. Thinking of him. It gets me thinking of the fact that there will soon be a physical distance between us too. It feels like a gut punch, not to see that face every day.

'When will I see you again?' I ask.

'We can meet if we are careful,' she says. 'If anything goes wrong, or there's an emergency, just call. We'll be monitoring you through the tracker anyway, and once we fit the pigeon camera you'll be able to communicate with us whenever you like. Of course, it's a one-way relay, as in you can talk to us but there's no earpiece so we can't talk to you. You can just tell me where and when and I'll be there. And I'll see you at the Feathers Ball.'

'I'll save a dance for you,' I joke.

'You'd better save more than one, Eddie,' she says, not joking. 'It's going to be our one legitimate meeting. If we need to catch up outside of that, we're going to have to do so in secret.' She scrapes the coffee foam from her cup. 'There's one more thing. We have to start calling you Brat. It has to be as if you are him. *You* have to believe you are him.'

I nod.

We stand up to leave. I have to catch a bus to New Haven, Harper has to go back to Ida Barney. I pick up my suitcase. It's packed carefully with purchases from the weekend – all the things I will need for the first night: monogrammed pyjamas, a silk dressing gown, slippers and a wash bag. My other things, the casual clothes, the formal clothes, the spare uniform, have been sent on ahead in a trunk marked BVB in discreet gold letters.

Harper doesn't quite meet my eyes. She looks as if she's deciding something. Then she looks at me with that very direct blue gaze. 'One thing I have to reiterate,' she says, low voiced. 'And this is the last time I'll talk of Brat in the third person. Brat Van Buren was a confident boy – it was ingrained in him from being born of centuries of privilege. But the last time I saw him he was afraid. *Really* afraid.' She leans in and quickly kisses me on the cheek. It feels like there's a certain circularity to the beginning and to the end of this chapter of our acquaintance – what began with a slap ended with a kiss. 'Good luck, Brat.'

And with that she is gone.

I look again at my new self in the mirrored wall of the café. Now, of course, I look afraid too. But I stand a little straighter, raise my chin an inch, steady my gaze. I need some of that bred-in-the-bone confidence. And it works. I think I do see a new light of determination in my amber eyes.

Goodbye, Eddie Dontay.

Hello, Brat Van Buren.

There are pigeons everywhere I go.

I'd never really noticed pigeons before but now I do. Grey, utterly commonplace, so ubiquitous you don't see them. Cooing constantly, but you never hear them. Pottering and pecking and fluttering for centuries. Beneath everyone's notice, but at the same time utterly integral to New England society.

A bit like me.

But then I correct myself. Eddie Dontay is dead. I am now Brat, and I must remember that. I am Brat. *I am Brat.* I find myself scrabbling beneath my white cravat for the gold Van Buren medallion. For a moment it works its metallic magic – warm to the touch, it centres me, calms the panic, reminds me who I am.

I walk down the drive to the school, scattering the pigeons as I go. New Haven. Founded in 1635, added to over the centuries to make a pleasing muddle of architectural styles – of course, Harper's been showing me photos for weeks, but it's so different seeing the place for real. Dominant over all is the high Gothic, red bricks that rise to the sharp pinnacles of the chapel, piercing the blue sky like thorns. It's every building in every novel I've read in the past two weeks. It's Northanger Abbey, it's Thornfield Hall, it's Castle Dracula. Yes, there are green lawns, yes, there are the staple New England trees with their fiery fall foliage, but everything seems looming and dark and unmistakably Gothic. The bells begin their carillon marking the hour, and suddenly everything is real. My heart hammers in time with the chimes. I'm going to walk into this school as Brat Van Buren, and then there's no going back.

Exactly as the chapel bell strikes nine, my knuckles meet the oaken door of the principal's office. Dr Bretton Gordon, a lifelong academic with steel-grey hair and glasses, dressed in black, actually gets up from his desk to shake my hand. I hope mine isn't damp.

'Welcome back, son,' he says. 'I trust you had a good sabbatical and have returned ready to learn?'

'Yes, sir,' I say.

'Mr Seamark wrote to me of your return. Your fees will be carried over from last year. I assume that you are waiting for your great-aunt's estate to be administered.' He looks at me keenly from behind the horn-rimmed glasses. 'May I offer you my condolences on the passing of your aunt. Bunny Van Buren was an extraordinary woman.'

Suddenly I feel tears prick at the back of my eyes. Boy, I'm really in character.

He sees the emotion and reacts in the classic New England way, by clearing his throat gruffly and clapping me on the shoulder. 'Well. Well. We'll say no more about it. A new start, eh?'

'Yes, sir,' I say for the second time.

'Good, good. Well.' He consults a page on his desk. 'You're due in class. It's literature, with Professor Walpole.'

*Literature.*

There is to be no time, it seems, for adjustments. From the café to the classroom – I am going straight from the frying pan into the fire.

## 5

I'm thinking, as I open the door to Professor Walpole's classroom, that I've never done anything more terrifying in my life. But then I remember.

I have.

Much, *much* worse.

And if I can come back from that I can come back from this.

I push open the heavy door, and every eye turns towards me. Time slows and sticks and stops. My panicked brain turns to analytical mode, and I take a mental register of the characters before me.

Professor Lewis Walpole, bearded and tweeded, standing at the blackboard mid-thought, chalk in hand. *Check*.

Then The Gloomth members:

Ignatio Jorquera aka Iggy. Slim, with heavy brows and black curls. *Check*.

Oliver Arblaster. Bespectacled and preppy, and pale enough to be almost transparent. *Check*.

Lowell Bell-Cross. Athletic and WASPy, tall, broad and all-American. *Check*.

And there, right at the front of the class like a ship's figurehead, *he* is.

Ulysses Parslow. *Check*.

He is the last one to turn, so for a moment I can see his exquisite profile, pale and perfect like he is etched in marble. His hair is even darker than Iggy's, but with an extra hue, the blue-black of a raven's wing. It falls in waves around his face, and when he turns I can see his eyes, silver grey like a wolf's. His cheekbones are pronounced, as if he is starved by melancholy, and his skin is even paler than Oliver's. His has something of the grave about it, a grey pallor. Looking at him like that, as if for the first time, I can see that he is simultaneously the most beautiful and the most terrifying human I have ever met.

I look at them all, the members of The Gloomth, who stand out from their fellows as if they are carved in relief. I don't look at the other dozen or so boys in the class, just at them. So different from each other, but they all share one thing.

They look petrified.

And I mean that in the literal sense of the word. They look as if they have been turned to stone. But instead of resembling Greek statues, they look more like gargoyles, with expressions of utter terror etched on their faces. When the moment breaks, they look at each other in horror.

I feel a fire ignite inside me. I'm glad. Glad I can make them fearful. For a moment I am not afraid – I feel like a cat among the pigeons.

As they unfreeze, Lewis Walpole comes towards me as if in a dream. He extends his hand to clasp mine, and his is shaking. But not from fear. He looks at me with wonder, as if I am some legend stepped from myth. It's almost as if he can't believe I'm real until he has touched me. I look at his face, trying to gauge his reaction. The cheeks above the white beard are flushed and a little spark dances in each water-green eye. The mouth curls beneath the white moustache. And at last I can decode his expression.

Joy.

Lewis Walpole is many things. Surprised, intrigued, flummoxed. But above all, joyous. He is *glad* to see me. Fascinated. Alive.

'Bless my soul,' he says appropriately. 'Bartholomew Van Buren, as I live and breathe.'

I continue the theme of the tomb. 'In the flesh,' I say. 'How are you, sir?'

'Well, well.' I can't tell if it's an answer or an exclamation. He walks all around me, like I'm a car he's buying. There's a certain wariness to his tread, as if he's not entirely sure what I'm going to do.

'You were not expecting me?' I ask. I would have thought that Dr Gordon would have warned him that I was returning to class. Apparently not.

'Certainly not,' he says. 'But I can assure you this is a . . . pleasant surprise. I have missed your contributions in class. I recall one particularly spirited discussion about whether or not *The Count of Monte Cristo* qualified as a Gothic novel.'

This is something that Harper left out of her tuition, presumably because she didn't know about it. But Eddie Dontay recalls a furious discussion at Marty's Café between Stacey and Domingo the meat guy about whether *Die Hard* is a Christmas movie. I think the *Monte Cristo* conversation must be a more intellectual version of that. It is time to be Brat – to show some confidence and treat the professor as an equal. 'And have you revised your opinion, sir?'

'Do you know?' he says, getting very close to me and looking me in the face. 'I rather think I have.'

For a moment we lock eyes. He looks quizzical and amused, I'm trying to look entitled and entirely comfortable. Then he snaps to himself and claps his hands together. They sound to me like thunder. 'Now,' he says. 'If Mr Van Buren would oblige us by taking a seat, we may proceed with today's class. And as always at the beginning of our course of study, we start with the very first Gothic novel, *The Castle of Otranto*.'

Then an odd thing happens. All the boys, every last one of them, start cooing like pigeons. In another setting it might have been comedic, and indeed Lewis Walpole does start to smile. The sound chills me to the very marrow of my bones. I know what it means. Harper didn't know why the emblem of The Gloomth was a pigeon, but I knew as soon as I saw the title of the first ever Gothic novel. *Castle Of Otranto*. COO. The pigeon was a reference to the book that began it all, authored by Sir Horace Walpole, the man who invented the word *Gloomth* and was the direct ancestor of our English professor.

As the cooing subsides, I take the seat Lewis Walpole indicates with his chalk – up at the front of class right next to Ulysses Parslow. The professor finishes writing the title on the blackboard, in that strange archaic way where the Ss have long tails and look like Fs.

## *The Caſtle of Otranto*

Lewis Walpole bangs a copy of the book down in front of me, just like Harper did in the library.

'Walpole's novel introduces key elements of Gothic literature,' he begins. 'These include the use of ancient settings, supernatural occurrences, the sublime, and the exploration of the human condition through terror and mystery. It also treats on themes of inheritance, fate and hubris.' He looks round the room, capturing all of us with his glance, and settling on me. '*The Castle of Otranto* outlined the parameters for the genre; its unique blend of horror, romance and the macabre set the stage for a wide range of literature that followed down the ages.'

For the rest of the period I am set the nigh-on impossible task of concentrating on the convoluted story, while feeling the eyes of the Gothic Boys boring into my back. And every time I look up, the silver-grey eyes of Ulysses Parslow are looking at me with wonder and terror. In the end I get sick of it and meet his eyes. He drops his gaze first.

As I leave class the others avoid me in the doorway, as if I am infected. I follow the flock of boys down the ancient cloister to my next class, and I see the four Gothic Boys huddle together, talking intently, heads close. Now and again they shoot a glance behind them to check that I am real. And I am. I definitely am.

As I tread the ancient pavings I rehearse in my head how I will describe that first encounter to Harper. It occurs to me exactly how I will express the reaction of The Gloomth to my reappearance.

It was as if they had seen a ghost.

Somehow I stumble through the rest of the day's lessons. I spend my time in class putting faces to names. Of course I 'know' all these boys from the year before, and Stevie had accessed a class roll to remind me. There are two new boys – fiery red hair: Jess Emerson. West Point buzz cut: Calvin Southern. But what I can't avoid are the four Gothic Boys, huddled together in their own row. And watching. Always watching.

When I finally fall into bed, I am mentally exhausted but can't sleep. The dormitory is comfortable and pleasant with my dorm-mates around me but there are four empty beds in here and those gaps, like missing teeth, pain me and keep me awake. Do The Gloomth live someplace else, or are they wakeful somewhere, engaged in some dark ritual? I get up and pad to the library in my slippers. Well briefed, I can find it easily even in the dark. Compared to the dormitory the cavernous gloomy library holds no fears for me. I click on a single desk lamp and search the shelves for the book I want – I find it as the gold letters sing out at me. *The Count of Monte Cristo.* Time to study.

As I tread back to the dorm, I pass the door of the chapel and I hear whispering voices. I flatten myself against the cold wood and peep round – the four Gothic Boys are sitting in the front pews. Alongside them is a white head: Lewis Walpole. I search my brain for an innocent reason for this particular collection of people to be meeting in the dead of night and come up with nothing.

Heart hammering, I slip inside. I know the geography of the chapel, thanks to Harper, like the back of my hand, and I happen to know that by the huge and ancient pipe organ there is a confessional box, a vestige of the days when New Haven was a Catholic seminary. I creep inside and noiselessly shut the door, then peer through the dark-wood grille deep into the gloom of the chapel. My ears are tingling, straining for every whispered word. I've obviously joined the conversation halfway through. Ulysses Parslow is speaking and his voice sends a shiver through me.

'But how is it possible?'

'I thought you were sure,' says Iggy.

'I *was* sure,' Ulysses shoots back.

'But that is just what makes the whole situation so intriguing,' says Professor Walpole. 'You *did* make sure. And yet here he is. He has returned.' He gets to his feet and I see him take a pipe from his pocket. He strides to the altar, picks up a candle and lights the pipe, puffing out a cloud of smoke that rises to the vaulted ceiling like incense. He obviously has no heed for whose house he is in, and I suspect that Lewis Walpole worships older gods. He stands in the apse for a moment, gazing up at the crucifix over the altar. 'There could hardly be a more apt place to meet,' he says. 'Our friend pulled off a trick worthy of Jesus Christ himself.'

'This is no time for theology,' spits Ulysses.

'He's right,' says Lowell. 'What are we going to *do*? I have my Harvard entrance next semester.'

'And I've got Yale,' says Oliver. 'I don't need a scandal.'

'There will be no scandal,' says the professor with a chilling certainty to his voice.

'I can't believe it. I won't believe it. It's some imposter. It *can't* be him.' Ulysses is adamant.

'Oh, it's him all right,' says Lewis Walpole. 'He's back.' He throws back his head and laughs – he's enjoying this. 'Don't you all feel alive too?'

The Gothic Boys look at each other, troubled, perplexed, afraid. No one answers.

'Boys, boys,' says Lewis Walpole, walking among them like Henry V, touching a shoulder here, a cheek there. 'Don't you see? This is thrilling. At some level, our strange practices have worked. There could scarcely be a better outcome for a society that celebrates the macabre. This whole episode is *entirely* Gothic, in the truest sense. Feel afraid. Feel terrified. Quake. Shudder. Cry. This, *this* is Gloomth.'

'Then what do we do?' asks Ulysses. 'Do we pledge him?'

'But of course,' says the professor, drawing on his pipe. 'If only to see if it happens again.'

'And if it doesn't?' says Oliver.

'Then the school benefits. Bunny Van Buren is dead, Brat's parents died in a car crash and he is the only heir.' The way he says this, so suddenly, is like being doused in icy water. 'Old Jeremiah Van Buren was a Gloomth member, and he willed his fortune to the school if there are no living male heirs. But you know all this,' he says. 'Now, I must to my bed. And you, boys' –

he collects them with a glance – 'you know what you must do.' Then his voice changes, as people's do when they are quoting. 'Remember that what has once been done may be done again.' It sounds like a line from a novel. And of course, that's exactly what it is.

The members of The Gloomth look at each other and nod. They get up and walk out of the door, an order of sinful monks, their slippers soundless on the marble floor, their silk dressing gowns billowing behind them, the candle flames bending as they pass.

When they have gone, the professor knocks out the innards of his pipe into the font – the ashes of the risen Christ. He stands, contemplating the god that is not his, for a long moment before he too leaves the place. Only then do I let my head fall back against the wood of the confessional. My heart hardens. Proof. *Proof.* I wish I had Anna's camera already. I would have been able to record evidence that something shady was going on. But the encounter hasn't been a waste. My suspicion that The Gloomth are up to something has been confirmed, and I've only been here a day. I look at the book in my hands, some trick of the candlelight turning the gold lettering to fire. THE COUNT OF MONTE CRISTO. The book Brat – I – thought was a Gothic novel, and Lewis Walpole didn't.

I'm about to prove Brat right.

When it's safe, I slip out of the confessional and leave the chapel. It suddenly becomes hugely important that I am in bed before the Gothic Boys are. I skid along the passageway to the back stairs, the ones built back in colonial times for the servants, and hurry back to the dormitory. Four beds are still empty. I hide *The Count of Monte Cristo* under my pillow and lie on it. It presses against my head, hard and enduring, like a vow.

# PART 3

## The Tell-Tale Heart

'Villains!' I shrieked. 'Dissemble no more! I admit the deed! Tear up the planks! Here, here! It is the beating of his hideous heart!'

*The Tell-Tale Heart* – Edgar Allan Poe, 1843

# 1

It turns out that terror is tiring. I do eventually sleep, waking with the rising bell. Hollow-eyed, I go down to breakfast and have to force myself to eat. I grab a bagel and attempt to wash it down with some coffee. I sit on my own at the end of a long refectory table. No one comes near me, as if I have my own personal forcefield. The seclusion is not necessarily hostile. Suddenly I miss Harper with the force of a blow.

At least my outcast status gives me a chance to look around in peace. The room has high Gothic ceilings and dark oak panelling studded with the pictures of past principals in their academic gowns. Arched crystal windows look down the rolling green bank to the river, where early morning rowers flick past, oars shallow. I don't fully know my schedule yet, so I realise I have forgotten the academic gown I need to wear for Convocation – which is what New Haven call their assembly. I race up to the dormitory to grab it, so I don't have to suffer the indignity of going into the chapel late and having the eyes of the school drawn to me even more than they already are.

I don't notice the object on my bed at first. I'm too busy rummaging in my locker for my gown. But when I turn, I see a wreath on my bed.

A funeral wreath.

Suddenly icy cold, I approach it. The wreath is a multi-layered circle of leaves – laurel, I'm guessing, like Caesar's crown – and it has a picture of me in the middle with *RIP* inscribed in black calligraphy. A black ribbon is tied in a flourishing bow at the base. And at the top, pinned to the greenery, is a scroll.

So it begins.

With a shaking hand, I take out the pin and unfurl the paper.

*The lower part of the castle was hollowed into several intricate cloisters; and it was not easy for one under so much anxiety to find the door that opened into the cavern. An awful silence reigned throughout those subterraneous regions, except now and then some blasts of wind that shook the doors she had passed, and which, grating on the rusty hinges, were re-echoed through that long labyrinth of darkness. Every murmur struck her with new terror; yet more she dreaded to hear the wrathful voice of Manfred urging his domestics to pursue her . . .*

It's handwritten in calligraphy, and it's made more difficult to read by the fact that, again in that strange archaic way, the Ss have long tails and look like Fs. My racing eyes recognise the type of writing a second before I recognise the passage. It's from the book we've just been studying – the same book that I read in the Washington Library, the book that started this whole thing.

*The Castle of Otranto.*

It's the part where Manfred, the evil lord of Otranto, pursues his young runaway bride into the bowels of the cursed castle. She hides in the subterranean crypts, vowing to join an order of nuns rather than marry a tyrant.

I turn the paper over. On the back it says:

*Midnight: chapel crypt*
*Know this passage BY HEART*

*By heart* is capitalised and underlined three times. They mean it.

Now The Gloomth have decided to pledge me, they are not wasting any time. I hide the wreath under my bed but the paper I take with me – if I need to be off book by tonight, I'll have to learn it in any spare moments. I roll up the paper to put in my pocket and I see a streak of red on the scroll. The pin has pierced my flesh and there's a bright bead of blood on my finger.

I get the feeling that this is only the beginning of the bloodletting.

I end up late for chapel Convocation after all, and everyone does stare. In Convocation, Dr Gordon does the standard academic address about working hard and aiming high. I don't really listen but feel instead the crackle of paper at my thigh, where the scroll rests in my pocket. By tonight I have to know every word. The chapel looks like an entirely different building to the one I snuck into last night. This morning it is beautiful as the light streams through the stained glass.

That day I don't learn much in my classes. At every moment I study the passage from *The Castle of Otranto* and try to commit it to memory. As Harper rightly said, knowing what passage they set last year would not have helped me one jot, as it changes every time. There were as many options for this first pledge as there were paragraphs in the book. So I hide the scroll in my *Latin Unseen*, my logarithm tables and my anatomy textbook, mouthing the words to myself like a spell. Mr Margrave, the biology teacher, calls on me.

'Mr Van Buren.' His voice penetrates my Gothic daymare. 'What did I just say?'

I'm pulled back to reality. I blink at the picture in my anatomy book, and the corresponding picture on the chalkboard. 'The heart?' I say hopefully.

'Yes,' he says patiently. 'What about it?'

It's time to admit defeat. 'I don't know.'

Mr Margrave huffs out a windy sigh. 'I was *saying* that the aorta, the pulmonary artery and the superior vena cava are the three great vessels of the heart. As they leave the heart, the pulmonary artery is on the right, the superior vena cava to the left and the aorta in the middle, which is the largest and most important blood vessel in the body. Has that sunk in, Mr Van Buren?'

'Pulmonary artery on the right, superior vena cava on the left, aorta in the middle,' I say. 'Got it.'

Mr Margrave eyes me and moves on to another victim.

At some point in the day, I realise I am not alone in my endeavours. I notice that Jess Emerson, of the red hair, and Calvin Southern, of the flat-top buzz cut, are also nervously mouthing words to themselves, like ill-prepared actors on opening night. That makes three of us, and three makes sense, as a trio of Gloomth members left at the end of last year, no doubt carrying their Gothic gospel to the Ivy League establishments of the east coast. Harper told me The Gloomth always numbers seven, so we were the new initiates, the baby pigeons, the Squabs.

By bedtime I think I am word perfect, and I am mentally exhausted, but I know that I won't sleep. If there is a person who could rest effectively for a couple of hours and then wake ready for a pledge as crucial as this one, I would like to meet them, because I am certainly not able to. I lie awake, staring at the dormitory ceiling. It is a filthy night outside the windows, and the branches paw and skitter at the glass like claws. I am conscious once more that there are four empty beds, but tonight there are also three of us wakeful and twisting in our cots, while the same Gothic words march through our poor brains.

Unable to stand it any more, I rise well before midnight and don my dressing gown and slippers. Just like last night I pad down to the chapel, but this time with the scroll screwed up in my palm. The other two will have the extra challenge of trying to find the crypt, but I know the location by heart. Brat told Harper before he realised he wasn't supposed to talk about it.

I recall an exchange I once had with Harper. 'Think of Edgar Allan Poe,' she'd said one day in the library. 'What happened in *The Tell-Tale Heart*?'

I'd taken a deep breath. 'An unnamed narrator is driven to madness by the way a man is looking at him. He plans and carries out the man's murder, cutting up the body and hiding it under his floor. The murderer tries to live his life as normal, but he becomes increasingly convinced that he can hear the dead man's beating heart through the boards.'

Now, treading through the chapel in the dead of night, I think again about *The Tell-Tale Heart*. When I'd read it, I'd thought it a creepy and effective story, but I'd never really bought that a man could be driven to murder just by the way someone looked at him. Now, having endured just twenty-four hours under the silver-grey eyes of Ulysses Parslow, I can well believe it. He'd not yet addressed me directly, just looked. Everywhere I went, his eyes followed me. In the story, Poe called it 'the vulture eye' and he was absolutely right. There is something predatory about the way Ulysses looks at me – like how a hawk looks at a baby pigeon.

The candles are all lit in the chapel – we are expected. By the light of a thousand tiny flames I tread down the nave, searching for the Tell-Tale Heart. I don't see any doors, but this doesn't bother me – Harper told me what to look for. On the far wall is a fresco of the life of Christ and I walk over to it. In the wavering candlelight I look at the frieze. Of course, I know all about it – painted in 1790 by Jeremiah Waterlow, a New Haven alumnus who joined the Royal Academy in London. I walk along the timeline, from birth to death, Nativity to Crucifixion, and at last I find what I'm looking for. Jesus, in the kingdom of heaven, wearing the dress code of white robes. His face is serene and glowing, but his heart is on fire. I get closer. The heart is painted outside the robes, wreathed in flame, encircled by a crown of thorns and pierced by a lance. Christ's wounded hands point towards the heart, showing me the way. I press my fingers to the sacred heart and a panel opens inwards, swinging silently on an unseen hinge, revealing a spiral staircase. My own heart pounds.

If I'm right about the other two, Jess and Calvin, I wonder how they will find this door without my own advantage of knowing how Brat got here the year before. Then I open my palm and smooth out the paper I've been given. I look at the instruction that was capitalised and underlined three times.

## *BY HEART*

The door is by the heart.
Clever.
I place my slippered foot on the first stair and descend.

It's colder on the staircase than in the chapel, but it's not all dark. Torches are set into the walls at intervals, and I can't escape the feeling as I descend that I'm spiralling downward through time and I will emerge into some medieval castle. Maybe the Castle of Otranto. At the bottom of the stairs there is not one way forward but three. Identical archways lead off into a fork of identical passageways, all torchlit, all inviting me in. I hesitate, not knowing which one to take – in the end I take the left. I wander around for some time, in a maze of passageways.

I'm glad I came early. I thought this might happen. Sometimes I think I hear voices, whispers in the dark places beyond the light, but then I think my mind is playing tricks and it is just the hissing of the torches.

At last I think I've come to the centre of the labyrinth, but I realise with dismay that I am back at the foot of the staircase. I could wander here for hours and still not find the lair of The Gloomth, and miss my chance to be pledged. I think again about the other two hopefuls, and how they will find their way. But then I realise I have no real advantage – even if you'd trodden these paths before there would still be no way of remembering the right way through the darkness. I try again, this time determining at each parting of the ways to take a different passage to the one I took before. Where I took the left before, I now take the right. Then I mix it up a bit. But it's no use. Two, three times I end up in the same place. I am the hapless Isabella, trapped in the 'dark labyrinth' of dungeons beneath the Castle of Otranto, doomed to wander forever. I look at the paper in my hand as if the answer might be there. I have an idea. This time as I walk, I recite the passage from *The Castle of Otranto* to myself.

I speak the words over and over. I can't let fear push it from my memory. I have to get that silver pigeon skull, and I have to get it tonight. My own voice comforts me, and the words of *The Castle of Otranto* keep pace with my footsteps. My heart beats in my ears like a metronome, I think of nothing else but the lines, and don't try to find my way. I feel as if some alchemy might guide me to the centre, that the long-dead Horace Walpole might reach out his spectral hand across the centuries and lead the way. But it's of no use. Once again, I am back at the foot of the staircase.

Desperate, I look again at the scroll. This time I turn the paper over.

## *Know this passage BY HEART*

I look at the words in the torchlight. Suddenly the message means something else. Sure, 'By heart' was the clue to the sacred heart and the door into the dark. But 'know this passage' suddenly seems to mean something else. It doesn't mean a paragraph of a book, but a physical corridor, a geographical term, not a literary one. But how to find the right passage of three?

*By heart.*

Suddenly I'm back in today's biology lesson. What if it wasn't an accident that Mr Margrave was teaching us the three great vessels of the heart this morning? And when he noticed me not listening and called me out on it, he'd made me recite those vessels back to him. But that would mean the whole school was in on this Gloomth thing. I check myself. Of *course* they are all in on this Gloomth thing. Lewis Walpole said only last night, in this very chapel, that if whatever happened to me last year happens to me again 'the school benefits'.

So I look again at the three passageways in front of me and try to recall the words from my biology lesson. *The aorta, the pulmonary artery and the superior vena cava. As they leave the heart, the pulmonary artery is on the right, the superior vena cava to the left and the aorta in the middle*, which is the largest and most important blood vessel in the body.

In the middle.

It's worth a try.

This time I take the middle way, and each time I'm presented with a choice, always of three passageways, I take the middle one. And although it seems unbelievable that New Haven might have constructed a subterranean maze, centuries ago, based on the newly discovered anatomy of the human heart, this time I find myself in a wide round chamber, encircled by torches. Waiting there, watchful as always, is Ulysses Parslow, looking like the prince of the underworld, flanked by his acolytes: the members of The Gloomth.

# 4

I notice in the shadows the two other boys – Jess and Calvin. By accident or design they've got here before me, even though I left first.

Silently I go over and join them. They are both in pyjamas, slippers and dressing gowns too. And although my outfit is more expensive and more elegant than anything I ever wore as Eddie Dontay, my fellow Squabs and I form a marked contrast to the members of The Gloomth: Ulysess, Oliver, Lowell and Iggy.

They stand like Roman soldiers going into battle, with Ulysses Parslow at the front. They are immaculately dressed in their Gloomth uniforms, looking – appropriately – like some kind of Edgar Allan Poe tribute act. Their attire consists of a black tailcoat and snowy-white shirt with a white cravat knotted high around the throat. The cravats are fastened with silver tie pins fashioned in the form of a pigeon skull, all with the sharp beaks pointing to the right. I gaze at the nearest silver skull. I can't leave this chamber without one. The whole plan rests within one of those little silver craniums.

And it seems the time is at hand. The Gloomth part to reveal three podiums. Each one has a parchment resting on it, and on top of the parchment, a silver pigeon skull, beak pointing to the left.

'Approach your pact,' says Ulysses Parslow, making a sweeping gesture with his hand. 'And sign.'

Since the middle way has served me well tonight, I walk to the middle podium. Ulysses joins me to police the operation, while Oliver stands by Jess, and Lowell watches Calvin. Iggy disappears into the dark on other business and by the flickering torchlight I read the document – even the writing has the power to frighten me now, because it is the same calligraphy that was on the scroll in my pocket. The Ss look like Fs. The pact says:

> *I, Squab, do by this contract solemnly swear that all my dealings with The Gloomth shall be as silent as the grave. And that if I speak a word of what transpired between myself and the society, my life is forfeit.*
> *Signed:*

And then there's a gap at the foot of the parchment – space enough for a name.

'Now,' says Ulysses, 'take the skull in your right hand and pierce the pad of your left forefinger with the beak.'

I take the silver skull in my hand. It is cold to the touch. Only now do I notice that the beak is needle sharp. Suddenly shaking, I press the beak into my forefinger hard enough to break the skin. A bright bead of blood appears on my fingertip, just as it did when I pricked my finger on the pin from the scroll. I look left and right at my fellow Squabs. Jess looks relatively unconcerned by this act; strangely it is the burly Calvin who looks unsteady on his feet, like he might be about to faint. 'Dip the beak in the blood,' says Ulysses, 'and sign your name.'

This is a tricky business, and it takes me a few goes to form the letters. I have to squeeze my fingertip a couple of times to encourage more of the red ink. But at last, cursing the length of my family name, I form the final character, the final stroke of the three.

*Bartholomew Van Buren III*

I am now pledged in blood.

'Gentlemen. The skull is now yours. Do *not* wipe the beak.' And now I realise why I hadn't registered the sharpness of the beaks before. Each skull's beak is blunted by the blood of its owner. The point is still there, but it is wreathed in crusted blood.

'And do not tell a soul what passes here tonight,' Ulysses goes on. Then he leans to my ear, so close that I can feel the warmth of his breath. '*This time.*' There's a harsh emphasis to the whisper and I draw back and look at him sharply. He holds my gaze steadily and the grey eyes tell me that he knows – somehow – that Brat told Harper about the first pledge.

Before I can engage with the sheer impossibility of this, Iggy, the spare member of The Gloomth, comes forward from the shadows carrying three suits of clothes suspended from hangers. 'Here,' he says, 'are your uniforms.' He gives one to each of us. The clothes are heavy – the quality of good tailoring, heavy silks and wools, linings and layers, never one layer when two will do. These have the heft of rich people's clothes, a world away from the cheap, flimsy Target gear of Eddie Dontay.

'Put them on,' says Iggy.

It's an order. Jess, Calvin and I look at each other. It's immensely threatening having to strip butt naked under the eye of The Gloomth. I feel cold and vulnerable, like a baby. To have them all stare at us, at our flesh – there's something inhuman about it. We all dress as quickly as we can, covering the skin inch by inch. I realise I still have the scroll of the *Castle of Otranto* passage crumpled in my hand, so I slip it into one of my new pockets. The clothes are excellently cut, and fit so well that The Gloomth must have contrived to get hold of our exact measurements – most probably from the school tailor, a reminder of just how deep this thing goes.

By the time we are dressed we are all the same. The process feels transformative – I can see it in the others, feel it in myself. We all stand taller, the black coats hanging from shoulders that are somehow broader than before, backs that are straighter. The cravats are wound around necks that are more aligned, tied under chins that are higher. We've gone from babes to men in a matter of moments. The only difference between us Squabs and The Gloomth is the fact that our pigeon skulls point to the left, theirs to the right.

'Good,' says Ulysses, nodding approvingly. 'You're ready.'

We don't need to ask for what.

For the first pledge.

This time it is Oliver who disappears into the shadows. He reappears with a wooden drinks trolley. It is loaded with bottles that clink menacingly as he rolls it over the uneven stone. The Gothic Boys sit themselves in four oak chairs I hadn't noticed before, carefully placed below four torches so they are all illuminated in harsh shadow, like a merciless hanging committee.

Ulysses speaks.

'You are required to read from our sacred text, *The Castle of Otranto* by Horace Walpole. Any mistake, however small, will result in the penalty of imbibing one shot of absinthe. Absinthe, as you must know, has been the friend of scores of Gothic writers. Known as the Green Fairy because of its brilliant colour, it was popularised in the nineteenth-century Gothic coteries of Paris and London.'

I look at the bottles. I can't see the green in the torchlight – to me the bottles look like they are full of blood.

'Absinthe was banned in the USA in 1912 because of its strength and it is still prohibited by the FDA because it contains wormwood, a plant used for centuries as a medicine, an intoxicant and,' he pauses, 'a psychedelic.'

I swallow. Pack your bags, you're going on a trip. Oliver is pouring out little shot glasses. Ulysses takes the first one and raises it high. 'Gentlemen. One shooter to begin. We drink, as we always do, to Horace Walpole, with the traditional Gloomth toast: "Even in the Grave All is Not Lost".'

I take the little glass Oliver proffers. His hand is steady; my hand is shaking. Now, by some trick of the light, I can see the intense green, strong and slick and sticking to the sides of the glass.

'Even in the Grave All is Not Lost,' we repeat as one. I possibly say it a little louder than the others, as it's a saying in which I fervently believe. I down the drink – it is sweet and fiery and burns a trail to my stomach.

'First up,' says Ulysses, 'Mr Van Buren.'

Of course, I have an advantage. But I'm still nervous – even that one shot of absinthe has gone to my head and addled my senses, the Green Fairy flying through my veins and my brain. I feel an uneasy cocktail of euphoria and terror. For a moment I can't remember a single word of the passage. But then I close my eyes and the Green Fairy dances before my inner vision, leading me forward like Tinkerbell led Peter Pan. I'm lost in the dark labyrinth beneath the castle of Otranto, but I follow the little green light.

> *'The lower part of the castle was hollowed into several intricate cloisters; and it was not easy for one under so much anxiety to find the door that opened into the cavern. An awful silence reigned throughout those subterraneous regions, except now*

*and then some blasts of wind that shook the doors she had passed, and which, grating on the rusty hinges, were re-echoed through that long labyrinth of darkness. Every murmur struck her with new terror; yet more she dreaded to hear the wrathful voice of Manfred urging his domestics to pursue her . . .'*

All that repetition throughout the day, all that recitation in the passages of the crypt, has paid off. I say the lines perfectly.

I open my eyes to meet those of Ulysses Parslow. He looks disappointed, as if he had hoped for me to fail. But he nods once. 'Good,' he says curtly. Weak with relief I step back.

'Mr Emerson,' says Ulysses. I'm not concerned for Jess, who looks nerdy and studious and for all the world like a fellow who would be able to recite a passage of prose perfectly. And so it proves. Or very nearly.

*'The lower part of the castle was hollowed into several intricate cloisters; and it was not easy for one under so much anxiety to find the door that opened into the cavern. An awful silence reigned throughout those subterraneous regions, except now and then some gusts—'*

'Stop,' says Lowell. If Oliver is Mr Weights and Measures, Lowell is text support.

Jess looks to him, eyes puzzled. 'What did . . . ?'

'Blasts not gusts,' says Lowell, unsmiling. 'Take a shooter and begin again.'

Oliver hands Jess another shot. He drinks it, hands back the glass and takes a deep breath. Naturally I'm afraid of what another measure of that green gloop will do to his head, but he says the words perfectly second time around, and retreats into the shadows, his relief palpable.

'Finally, Mr Southern,' says Ulysses.

I'm a little worried for Calvin. He looks like a big jock to me. But I'm able to hope that I'm guilty of judging a book by its cover – his sheer bulk has obviously kept the worst effects of the absinthe at bay, and he rattles the first words accurately enough.

'*The lower part of the castle was hollowed into several elaborate—*'

'Stop,' says Lowell. 'Intricate, not elaborate. Take a drink and start over.'

Calvin does as he's told, coughing and spluttering as he chokes down the green liquid.

'*The lower part of the castle was hollowed into several intricate cloisters; and it was not easy for one under so much angst—*'

Lowell interjects again. 'Wrong,' he says. 'Anxiety, not angst. Drink and start again.'

Calvin takes the proffered glass and downs it. I notice his eyes are unfocused and his hand is weaving slightly. I have the feeling this is only going to get worse. I had one shot of the Green Fairy and I already feel wasted. Granted, Calvin is bigger and bulkier than me, but he's now had three. Yet he actually gets a lot further this time. Perhaps the Green Fairy is leading him too, and the alcohol has helped him to relax. I watch him intently, saying the words in my own head, willing him on, my eyes boring into him as if I might somehow transmit the lines from my brain to his.

'*The lower part of the castle was hollowed into several intricate cloisters; and it was not easy for one under so much anxiety to find the door that opened into the cavern. An awful silence reigned throughout those subterraneous regions, except now and then some blasts of wind that shook the doors she had passed, and which, grating on the rusty hinges, were re-echoed through that long labyrinth of darkness. Every moment—'*

I notice it a fraction of a second before Lowell. I groan internally and close my eyes.

'Stop,' says Lowell. 'Every murmur, not every moment.'

This time Calvin laughs and slaps his palm to his forehead. This is an absolute dumpster fire. He's already as drunk as a skunk – there's no way he's getting through this. For the next few rounds, he barely gets beyond a few words.

*'The lower piece of the castle—'*

'Stop. Part not piece. Drink. Start over.'

*'The lower part of the castle was burrowed—'*

'Stop. Hollowed not burrowed. Drink. Start over.'

*'The lower part of the castle was hollowed into several infinite cloisters—'*

'Stop. Intricate not infinite. Drink. Start over.'

At this point Calvin falls to his knees and his shoulders shake. I think he's laughing again but realise with horror that he's crying. He howls like a baby, and in between the sobs he begins to form words, like they're the first words he ever spoke. 'I want my mom,' he says.

That simple, childlike appeal is a scalpel to the heart. For a big guy like this to be broken to this extent, to be taken to the place in his soul where he will cry like a child for his mother, is unbearable. Jess and I exchange glances. This is horrible. They've wrecked him, this bright, lively young fellow with his neat haircut and his nice manners and his pristine uniform, coming to New Haven with such hope and promise. My own heart, auricles and ventricles and all, hardens inside of me, and my blood kindles with the fire of rage against The Gloomth.

I make an oath there and then – no one else will *ever* go through this. I will stop it if it takes the last breath in my body, the last beat of my tell-tale heart.

Unable to stand it any more, I blurt out, 'You have to stop this! You'll kill him.'

Ulysses stands up. 'Don't ever.' He spits at me. '*Ever*. Question the ways of The Gloomth.' He walks over to the kneeling, sobbing boy. Slowly, deliberately. Then he reaches out his long white fingers and touches Calvin's buzz cut. Tenderly.

'That's it,' he says, his voice shivered by something close to ecstasy. 'Cry. Cry. Now you feel it, don't you? This, *this* is Gloomth.' His words echo, uncannily, the words of Lewis Walpole the night before. Then his voice hardens again. 'Up,' he says. 'Up. Do it again. Stand tall like the New Haven man you are.'

But Calvin is beyond getting up.

'Let me help him,' I say.

Ulysses shoots me a look. 'Do it.'

I pull Calvin up and set him on his feet. His face is varnished with snot and tears and vomit and he wavers like a boxer who has just done ten rounds. I put my arm across his chest, but he just leans over it, vomiting at my feet. Then he stays down, folded like a rag doll. I have an idea. 'Let him say it like this, for pity's sake,' I say.

'Pity,' says Ulysses speculatively, as if he's never heard of the concept. 'Very well. I'll allow it.' He sits back down.

I turn Calvin to the wall, so he's facing away from the quartet of Gothic Boys. Holding him with one arm, I surreptitiously pull the scroll from my pocket and uncrumple the page under his face. It's risky, but it's the only way to save him. I give Calvin a little shake. 'Read it,' I whisper in his ear. 'Loud as you can. You can do this.'

'No,' he groans. 'Noooooooooooooo.'

It's hopeless. They'll kill him. Then I have a flash of inspiration, like a green sprite flitting from one synapse to another. 'Do it for your mom,' I say.

His words are slurred, his voice foghorn loud, but somehow he manages to recite the words, all his fluids falling on the paper as he reads. Then I let him go, easing him gently to the floor, crumpling the page sodden in my hand so they won't know.

Ulysses stands. He looks oddly thwarted, as if he'd wanted a different outcome. My God. He's even worse than Harper said.

'Gentlemen of The Gloomth,' he says shortly. 'This meeting is adjourned.' The torches are extinguished one by one and the members of The Gloomth sweep out of the room in a swirl of smoke. We Squabs are left in the choking darkness.

'Take his other arm,' I say to Jess. 'I know the way.' Calvin is an inert weight, and for a moment I worry that he is actually dead. But then as we move him, he begins to groan; an unearthly sound that echoes through the crypt like the lament of a soul in torment. Somehow we stumble back through the labyrinth, back through the chapel and back to the dorm.

As quietly as we can, we undress Calvin and put him back in his pyjamas. I roll him on to his side in case he vomits again, and Jess gets the trash can and puts it by the side of his bed, underneath his slack and spattered face.

Calvin's beautiful Gloomth clothes lie stained with vomit on the floor. Somehow seeing them so spoiled makes me sadder than anything else that happened tonight. Not knowing what to do with them I roll them up and put them in his hamper. I unpin the pigeon skull and put it on his bedside, next to a picture of a kindly-looking woman who must be Calvin's mother. I turn the beak away so the hollow eyes can't police his sleep. Only his mother should watch over him.

'Your mom would be proud of you,' I whisper.

He can't hear me.

# PART 4

## Frankenstein

'Anguish and despair had penetrated into the core of my heart; I bore a hell within me which nothing could extinguish.'

*Frankenstein* – Mary Shelley, 1818

# 1

When I float into consciousness in the morning to the sound of the waking bell, I have a small intense headache in my left temple, which I attribute to the Green Fairy. And if I feel like this, God only knows what Calvin feels like. I had one shot of absinthe. He practically had a bottle.

I sit up and look across at him. He's groaning and ruffling his bristly flat top. At least he's alive. I hadn't entirely discounted the notion that he might, in the dead of night, have turned on his back and choked on his own vomit. I pop a couple of Advil and am about to lie back down again and shut my eyes, in an attempt to get rid of the headache in the quarter-hour of respite before the rising bell, when I see an envelope at the foot of my bed. I pick it up and examine it. It is made of creamy paper, and it has a black border like mourning stationery. On the front my name is written in calligraphy.

My heart starts to thump. *What now?*

I open the envelope, fingers slick with sweat. Inside is a stiff card with a black border. It is printed with the words:

*You are cordially invited to:*
*THE SQUAB DINNER*
*Meet at seven of the clock tonight*
*At the tomb of Theophilus Eaton*
*Grove End Cemetery*
*Full Gloomth Formals Will Be Worn*

I know Grove End Cemetery very well as it's the oldest cemetery in New Haven, and lies next to the Yale campus. It has an enormous stone gateway fashioned – oddly – like an Egyptian temple. For years the Egyptian Gate has been at the centre of all sorts of rumours about hazing rituals at Yale – its macabre inscription 'The Dead Shall Be Raised' has made it an ideal venue for baby occultists to leave their offerings.

It's said, too, that there are miles of subterranean steam tunnels leading from the cemetery to Yale Medical School, and the graveyard itself fuelled the rumours by belching forth secrets of its own. It was once the burial ground for the victims of an epidemic of yellow fever, and as recently as a couple of years ago a tree fell over in a storm revealing a skeleton tangled in its roots. Although I knew some of the tombs there pretty well, I wasn't familiar with the tomb of Theophilus Eaton – but I knew about him because he'd been one of the figures I'd researched in Washington Library. He was one of the original pilgrims and the founder of New Haven School.

I throw back my covers and pad over to Calvin's bed. He's got an envelope too. I shake him gently by the shoulder.

'How you doing, champ?'

He answers me with a groan.

I wave the invitation under his face.

'Look. There's a dinner tonight, so you'd better get your shit together.'

We have Phys Ed first thing, and there's no way Calvin will make that, even though it's his favourite class.

'I'll get you out of gym,' I say, 'but you can't stay in bed. While we're rowing, you'd better get down to Jet Cleaners with the clothes in your hamper, because you'll need them for tonight. And then go to a diner and drink some black coffee and a lot of water. And eat a full breakfast: grits, gravy, the whole nine yards. You'll feel better by lunch.'

Calvin lies back down again with another groan. I can only hope that he threw up most of the absinthe, because the Green Fairy can obviously do a number on you. But as I go down to breakfast, I note that my own headache has completely gone.

I expect to eat breakfast alone, just like the day before. But my expectations are confounded. Jess sits by me, plonking down his tray.

'Pretty wild last night, huh?' he says. I don't even have time to respond to this staggering understatement before Iggy sits the other side of me. Lowell and Oliver sit across from me, then Ulysses Parslow himself sits at the head of the table, like the patriarch I suppose he is. All of the Gothic Boys are in their rowing gear, cream New Haven jumpers casually knotted about their broad shoulders. They look far less threatening than they did last night, clad in their full Gloomth formals. With their handsome faces, white smiles and floppy hair they look like a bunch of Abercrombie & Fitch models.

'No Calvin?' asks Lowell pleasantly.

'No,' I say. 'He's not feeling too clever this morning.'

'Well, he did have a skinful,' says Oliver, smiling wryly.

'What he needs,' says Ulysses, 'is a Prairie Oyster. He'll be a new man.'

'What's a Prairie Oyster?' asks Jess, obviously enjoying this new friendly dynamic.

'You take a raw egg yolk, Worcestershire sauce, then you splash in some hot sauce, sea salt and ground black pepper. Then you drink it all down and you're as right as rain.'

'Sounds gross,' says Jess.

'Oh, it is,' says Ulysses with a smile.

I look at them in turn incredulously. They are talking like we'd all had a night in a bar and Calvin had had one too many brewskis. Quite apart from the fact that we were four years too young to drink, absinthe wasn't exactly beer. It was highly toxic, potentially lethal. The talk turns to other things, and Iggy tells a story about going to the wedding of a member of the Spanish royal family during his summer vacation. It's one hell of an anecdote. Very funny. Everyone laughs.

This bonhomie continues throughout the morning. We all go out to the boathouse in the stunning New England morning – fresh and cold with bright sun. Jess and I are in an eight with the rest of The Gloomth and a couple of makeweights and a coxswain from another class. We all carry the long craft from the boathouse and float it on the river. I take my position at stroke and we cast off, slicing through the river at quite a lick.

I've rowed before; my muscle memory does not fail me and I trim my oar with the best of them. It's a peerless day and the water sparkles from our blades like diamonds. Ulysses is my stern partner, directly in front of me at number seven, so I don't have to suffer his glances. Instead, *I* do the watching – observing the muscle playing on his back at each stroke. And when we ship oars to spin the boat, he actually turns to talk to me, all pleasantries about mutual acquaintances. I think I acquit myself well, but I don't even think Ulysses is testing me. It feels more like he is just enjoying talking on his level, to someone who moves in the same social circles. It is the first time since coming to New Haven that I feel the full force of his charm. His silver eyes narrowed against the sun, his dark hair blowing back from that perfect face, his lopsided smile that reveals a single dimple – his charisma is palpable. For the first time, too, I wonder just how close he and Harper were as teens – who could resist him?

At the end of the session, we lift the boat from the water and carry it like pallbearers back to the boathouse. As the stern pair, Ulysses and I stay to stow the oars, and for a moment we are alone. He pauses in the doorway as if considering whether or not to say something, then turns. Against the bright day he is a silhouette, a black shadow. I can't see his expression, but I hear his words.

'I know you're not Brat,' he says pleasantly. 'You are an imposter. I don't know how you got here, or what you're doing. But I'll find out.' He claps me on the shoulder. 'See you later.'

I follow him out into the sunshine, but my enjoyment of the morning and the golden day evaporates. Now I can only anticipate the evening to come with utter dread.

Before we can go to the cemetery, there is the rest of the day to get through, and the curriculum is hardly designed to settle the Squabs' nerves. In the afternoon we have Gothic literature with Professor Walpole. He seems as benign and eccentric as ever, and doesn't seem to notice Calvin, who has now rejoined us, looking a little pale and hollow, and somehow . . . diminished. But I eye the professor with suspicion. I heard him two nights ago in the chapel, egging The Gloomth Society on. *You know what you must do . . .*

Today we are studying *Frankenstein*, one of the books I reread at Harper's suggestion. We read from the book in turn, and I marvel once again at the story of a monster stitched together from the bodies of the dead, reanimated to wreak havoc in the lives of those he touches. For a while I forget about the night to come, drunk on the words, the genius of Mary Shelley.

'Mr Van Buren, carry on for us,' says the professor.

I read the words of the monster:

*'My heart was fashioned to be susceptible of love and sympathy, and when wrenched by misery to vice and hatred, it did not endure*

*the violence of the change without torture such as you cannot even imagine.'*

I stop for a moment, feeling the impact of what I've just read with the force of a blow. It could have been written about me. I, too, have a changed heart. Mine, too, was wrenched by misery to vice and hatred, with unimaginable torture. I find it extraordinary that someone can put your heart on paper, that a long-dead writer can know exactly how that change in you feels. And even more extraordinarily, that the writer of *Frankenstein* was an eighteen-year-old girl, living in a time when girls were seen and not heard.

'Mr Van Buren? Cat got your tongue?'

This seems like a peculiarly Gothic and absolutely on-brand thing for Lewis Walpole to ask. It brings me to myself, and I swiftly edit my thoughts to a teacher-friendly version. I can't say the first part about the transformation of my own heart, as that would give too much away, but I can smarten up the second bit.

'I find the writing incredibly powerful,' I say truthfully. 'Especially as it was written by such a young woman, not even a woman living in our enlightened times when girls are free to be outspoken and forthright, but a young woman living in the repressive and patriarchal nineteenth century.'

Lewis Walpole points his chalk at me and nods vehemently.

'*Yes*,' he says. 'Precisely. And the engine of her writing was the strength of her feeling. She was violently in love – and I use the word advisedly – with the married poet Percy Shelley. When he became hers, the pair had a child who died, and she longed more than anything for their child to be alive again. *Frankenstein* was the expression of that wish. No: more than that. Her writing was almost a spell, an incantation. "The Dead Shall Be Raised". And you felt the strength of that. I'm impressed.' He turns to the blackboard and chalks 'The Dead Shall Be Raised', with a sweeping underline for emphasis.

'She was to experience that feeling one more time in her life. When Percy Shelley drowned, aged just twenty-nine, her grief was, literally, visceral. His heart was torn from his body, just as she felt her heart was torn from hers, and she carried it with her for the rest of her life. She wrapped it in one of his poems, an elegy called *Adonais*, which he wrote following the death of his friend John Keats. The poem mentions the heart seventeen times.'

'She sounds so strange,' says Calvin with a short laugh.

Lewis Walpole turns on him at once. 'You think so, Mr Southern? You find the idea of rising from the dead singular?'

'Outside of Our Lord Jesus Christ, yessir, I do,' he says.

'Well,' says the professor, 'I think you could do no better than to consult your fellow Squab on this matter.'

'Who, Jess?' Calvin says.

'No. Mr Van Buren.'

'Me?' I say, surprised.

'Of course. You, better than any, know that the dead can walk again.' He looks at me intently, with his bright eyes. I feel them boring into my very soul, peering into the darkness of my secret self. My own heart speeding, I present him with an innocent face.

'Why me?' I ask.

'Because of *The Count of Monte Cristo*, of course,' he says. 'Your favourite book, as you professed to me last fall. A man who is presumed dead and comes back to life to wreak revenge on those who wronged him.' My heart slows again. I feel sure that hadn't been what he was about to say.

'Anyway. Let us not go down that particular cul-de-sac again, lest we find ourselves repeating last year's conversation. We'll return to the text in hand.' He turns back to the class. 'Mr Arblaster?'

Oliver takes over reading duties, but I've stopped listening. I'm trying to place the quote the professor used, the one he's written on the board. *The Dead Shall Be Raised*. I know it's not from *Frankenstein*. Suddenly I remember. It's carved on the Egyptian Gate of the Grove End Cemetery, and I'll be walking through that gateway, under those words, tonight. My mind wanders out the window, and I watch the daylight bruise to dark.

The birds flutter and settle, and as the pigeons come home to roost, my fears do too.

# 3

We walk under the Egyptian Gate in the dead of night. The vast stone pillars, like the entrance to some great temple, are floodlit, so we can easily see the letters carved in shadow:

> THE DEAD SHALL BE RAISED

The four Gothic Boys and the three Squabs gather beneath the incantation. We are dressed in our Gloomth formals, complete with pigeon skull pins, and the black suits and the seriousness of our intent give us the air of a funeral procession. The gates to the main cemetery are locked, but Ulysses produces a key from somewhere – I get the feeling that no door in this town is locked to him. We all hold hurricane lanterns, and once inside the graveyard we light the candles and hold them high – there is no one here to question us but the dead.

I could probably, from my research, find my way to Theophilus Eaton's tomb on my own, but I'm pleased I don't have to. I'm glad of the company. Our solemn procession forms a marked contrast to the jocular nature of our morning rowing session, but we Squabs find silent solace in each other, and the events of the night before have made Calvin indebted to me for life. I've deliberately avoided Ulysses since the little scene in the boathouse, but in all our tiny encounters in the afternoon, heading through the same doorway, handing out maths books or passing in the cloister, he has been as natural and friendly to me as if it never happened. To the extent that I've begun to wonder if it really did.

Ulysses leads us through the dark and stops at a large tabletop tomb. This must be the one. We gather round it in a circle, lanterns aloft.

'We recite the inscription together,' commands Ulysses.

We all read the words carved in the stone: the Squabs haltingly, The Gothic Boys with more confidence:

> *Eaton so fam'd so wise, so just,*
> *The Phoenix of our world, here lies his dust,*
> *This name forget, New England never must.*

'And now,' he says incredibly, 'we lift.'

We have reached peak Gothic. Following his lead, we all lay our hands on the tabletop gravestone and shove. It makes a grating, booming noise as it shifts aside to reveal a stone stairway. From below there is a glow of light, and we descend one by one into the netherworld.

I don't know what I expected to be beneath this necropolis. Maybe an ancient crypt, like the one that lies beneath the chapel of New Haven School, or a dusty catacomb with skeletons protruding from the earth like weird roots. I certainly didn't expect the sight that greets us.

We are in a wide brick chamber with a number of tunnels branching off into the dark. But in the main atrium all is bright with dozens of freestanding candelabras, and a large dinner table with a snowy tablecloth set for seven. The table is bright with crystal, and in the mouth of one of the tunnels a string quartet is playing chamber music, and a coterie of waiting staff stand to attention, holding flutes of champagne on silver trays. Most bizarrely of all, a series of dark oak podiums are set around the room, and each one carries a glass case containing a stuffed pigeon. I detect that the Committee of Taste has been at work in here – this underground space has been transformed into a drawing room worthy of one of New England's great families. Bemused and not a little unsettled, I take one of the proffered champagne glasses and drink it a little too fast for etiquette.

'Gentlemen, please take your seats,' says Ulysses. There are little cards denoting our places, held in the beaks of little silver pigeons. Three each side – we Squabs on one and the Gothic Boys on the other. I notice with some disquiet that I have been placed next to Ulysses, who is at the head – for tonight I am his right-hand man.

With every course I expect something dreadful to be lying beneath one of those silver hoods. But each time I am pleasantly surprised. It's merely course after course of the most delicious food – New England clam chowder, scallops in chilli jam and then, for the main course, *of* course, pigeon breast in red wine jus. What else?

Once again there is alcohol, even though we are well underage. Not just the champagne, but wine with every course. Conscious that (according to Harper) the challenges change every year, I am wary of being spiked. A glass of blood, a roofie, some hallucinogen added to my glass. But each vintage is finer than the last – white for the fish course, red for the meat, dessert wine for pudding. And the company is even better than the wine. The charm of The Gloomth is at full wattage tonight. The Gothic Boys use every one of their social skills to put us Squabs at ease; they are witty, confident, entertaining. Their anecdotes – scandalous tales of princes and presidents, all meant to go no further than this subterranean citadel – are second to none. I supply my own shaggy dog stories, of the year I 'spent abroad' carefully recalling all the postcards Harper told me about, with places and dates. I tell tall tales of Mauritius and Goa, Bangkok and Dubai. They swallow every morsel, and we all have a whale of a time. And Ulysses never once lets the mask slip. He never once repeats, by so much as a word or a glance, that he has seen through me. That he knows who I really am, or rather, who I am *not*. He is far too skilful an operator for that.

Calvin seems completely taken in by this performance. He laughs uproariously and joins in the conversation with stories of his own, which seem to revolve around sporting high jinks at the Cape Cod Yacht Club or on the ski slopes of Vail. Even the shy Jess, after a few glasses, relaxes enough to share his experiences. His tastes are more cultural and he has a spirited discussion with Iggy about the New York Opera, of which his father is a patron.

My fear, which has completely dissipated throughout the evening, only returns when I notice that the string quartet and the staff have disappeared into the tunnels and not returned. Oliver, who seems to be the quartermaster on these occasions, serves the port himself. Then Lowell produces a wooden box of

Cubans, and all the Gothic Boys light cigars. I, alone, refuse. I know myself well enough to know Cubans make me sick. The sole observer through the cigar smoke, I regard them all with narrowed eyes. The fug is like some odd mist of time, and I can see, so very clearly, them all at fifty, the image of their fathers – with their hedge funds or Supreme Court chairs or blue-chip executive directorships. And then the whole infernal cycle starts again, and their own sons will be down here, scrabbling to become members of this malign little band of brothers. While they smoke, and joke, and I choke, I'm waiting. Something wicked this way comes. There hasn't been the sniff of a pledge all evening, but I know the night won't pass without a challenge. So I'm waiting for the other shoe to drop. And, at last, it does.

'And now,' says Ulysses Parslow, 'it is time for the Exchange of the Tears.'

# 4

Ulysses stubs out his cigar in a crystal ashtray.

'By tradition the Squab who wins the COO challenge – that would be you, Brat – exchanges his tears with one of The Gloomth. Tonight, that will be me.' He looks around the table. 'We are all, by now, friends. We have shared tales around this table that bond us. But now it is time to bare our most secret souls. The Exchange of Tears makes us more than friends, it makes us brothers. And it is a bond closer than blood. To be bonded by blood you only have to prick a finger – there is no emotional engagement required. But to weep, to *really* weep, requires emotional commitment, and vulnerability. You and I, Brat, will share the saddest moment of our lives, and welcome the release of tears.'

So now I get to pay the price for correctly reciting the passage from *The Castle of Otranto* at first try the other night. I'm now entering a one-on-one emotional fencing match with Ulysses Parslow. This is no accident – our ancestors have been doing this for centuries, and we are the latest young champions to ride into battle for our respective families.

'As you know,' says Ulysses, 'the word "Gloomth", first coined by Horace Walpole, means to embrace the melancholy. That is what we are going to do now. There is only one rule, that in order to leave this place, and return to the corporeal world, the tears must flow.'

I swallow, thinking hard. That change in my heart, which only Mary Shelley seems to understand, has hardened that organ, toughened it into a sclerotic fist of gristle. I don't know if I can feel any more, feel anything but hatred and revenge. I don't know if there are any tears left in me. There is some respite though. It seems customary, in this emotional face-off, that the full Gloomth member has the honour of going first.

Ulysses leans back in his chair and closes those extraordinary eyes. 'I was fifteen,' he says. 'We'd gone to family friends in Nantucket – the Larssons – for the Christmas vacation.'

I know where this is going. Harper had told me the sorry tale of Ulysses's sister and the ice. But now, it seemed, I was to hear it from a brother's point of view.

'The lake on the property had frozen and one morning – the day after Christmas – we went ice skating. It was me and my little sister Timmie; she was eight at the time. And the two Larsson kids – Harper, who was my age, and her brother Stellan. Harper – boy, you've never seen anything like this girl.' He looks straight at me, like a challenge. 'Beautiful as an angel. I was in love for the first time in my life.'

I'm taken aback by this disclosure – the sheer honesty of it, as piercing and bracing as a winter wind across a frozen lake.

'Anyway, we had a great time – it was so cold that year and the lake was frozen solid. I'd take every opportunity I could to hold Harper's hand, take her arm, pick her up if she fell over.

We'd been friends since we were little kids, but this Christmas felt different. Now we were both grown.'

I guess my musings about how close they had been were now answered.

'Then Stellan fell over and got all wet and started crying, and Harper took him back to the house. I took Timmie out on the ice, and we skated for a while. I told her to stay near the edges of the lake, where the ice was thickest. Then Harper came back and I went to see that everything was all right with Stellan. We got to talking and . . .' He stops and looks around at us. 'I've never told anyone this before. We kissed. It was my first kiss, my best kiss. And I admit, I forgot all about Timmie. All I could think was Harper, all I could feel was our lips touching. I don't know how long we kissed, standing there in the middle of the ice. Nothing could have torn us apart. Except for a scream.'

I look around the table. Everyone is rapt, listening. It's like we are ancients round a fire, listening to some myth of gods and monsters. But this is no fable. It's true.

'I knew it was Timmie. We rushed over to where she'd been skating, but there was just a hole in the ice, a void in the whiteness. You think stupid things at the moment of utter disaster, don't you? I remember thinking that hole was the blackest thing I'd ever seen – the absence of ice, the absence of Timmie. Harper ran for help and I lay on the ice and reached through the hole. But I couldn't find her. I don't know how long I lay there. The police and the EMTs fished her out. I remember her little orange coat, her little blue face. They had to prise me off the ice with warm water – I was frozen to it. I've never been warm again since.'

I look at the faces of the listeners. They are frozen too, in absolute horror.

'I didn't cry that day, or the next. I didn't cry until the funeral, when I saw the little box. Then I howled like a wolf.'

Those, I remember, were Harper's exact words about that day.

'I knew it was my fault. That kiss between me and Harper was the kiss of death. Timmie should never have been out on the ice alone. And I never told a soul until tonight.'

I watch the tears collect in his eyes, overflow and spill down his cheeks, like they'll never stop.

'That moment on the ice changed me. The black hole was punched through my soul that day. I've felt that absence ever since.'

I should feel sorry for him. Anyone would. Only a monster could hear this story and remain unmoved. But that monster is me. Like Mary Shelley's creation, my heart has hardened. And my heart hardens against Harper too. Why did she not tell me about the kiss? Was it because she felt responsible also, and was trying to forget the guilt? I watch Ulysses cry, in an ecstasy of melancholy. He is wallowing, embracing it, and I remember what Harper said of him at the funeral. That was when the tears came, at a time when a young man would normally do anything to conceal his grief from the other mourners.

Then something absolutely extraordinary and repulsive happens. First Lowell, then Iggy, then Oliver, crowd around their master and begin to lick up his tears. Emboldened, Calvin joins in, then Jess. It's like Ulysses is being devoured. As they all flock around him, their tongues flicking on his flesh, he opens his eyes and looks right at me. The sorrow is gone. He is all-powerful, enjoying himself. It's a challenge.

I sit unmoved and unmoving, dry with disdain. Ulysses waves back his acolytes with a long white hand. Still he looks right at me, his eyes mirrored with tears. 'Come,' he says. He beckons me over. 'Drink them before they dry.'

Nothing except my mission to bring down The Gloomth, and the need to complete this pledge, would induce me to obey. But I lean in, put out my tongue and briefly lick his cheek. The salt tastes bitter, like loathing. I'm the last to drink. When I'm done, he wipes his cheeks with the tail of his white cravat.

'Now you,' he says.

This is the real challenge, in the face of which pretending to have sympathy with Ulysses pales into nothing. I have to muster emotion about another life, another person. Who is Brat Van Buren? I think of the lifetime I now know as well as my own, of what would have hurt him most.

And I have it.

I take a breath. There is no sob story, no setting of the scene, no pay-off. I make a single, bald statement, a solitary sentence.

'The thing for which I will never forgive myself,' I say, 'is that I missed my Aunt Bunny's funeral.'

In the end I don't have to act. My sorrow, my sympathy for that version of Brat, the one who was lost never to return, does the trick. I feel how much missing his great-aunt's funeral would have hurt him. A single tear falls from my left eye, the one nearest Ulysses. 'Mine,' he says, like he's playing doubles at the club. Quick as a cat, he bends to my cheek as if to kiss, and I feel his warm tongue lap up my tear. My insides shrivel with disgust. He looks into my eyes and I look into his. Did he look at Harper like this, on the ice that day? He's right, something has changed between us. A new bond has been formed. But it is not love. It is hate, as dark and deep as the grave.

Until that moment I hadn't understood just how close those two things are.

The bell in the Gothic spire of the cemetery chapel is striking the witching hour as we emerge from the underworld. We lift Theophilus Eaton's gravestone back into place, and my arms feel like noodles. I am wrung out by emotion. If I can feel so drained from one tear, how must Ulysses feel, after that torrent of Gloomth?

We light the lanterns again and make our way to the Egyptian Gate. It feels like I'm almost out of danger, that there is just one more netherworld portal to pass through before I'm free of this place. But the worst is yet to come. Something stands in our way, something terrifying.

There are three little gods standing in the gateway, barring our way like knee-high guardians of the underworld. As we draw closer, we can see that the figures have animal heads – one a ram, one a hawk and one a long-nosed jackal. They look absolutely fitting standing under the architrave of an Egyptian temple.

'These are canopic jars,' says Ulysses, who seems quite recovered from his tempest of tears. 'They were used by the ancient Egyptians during the mummification process, to preserve the organs removed from the body. There is one for each of you, Squabs. Open your jar and take out what is inside. Surrender your lanterns. You will need both hands.'

I give my lantern to Oliver, while Lowell and Iggy take those of the other Squabs. Then Calvin, Jess and I stand in front of our respective jars. Mine is the one with the head of a hawk – I look at him and he looks back at me with the hunger of a raptor. His sharp little face reminds me of the pigeon skull I wear at my throat. Our relative sizes don't seem to matter at all – he is the powerful one. Ulysses produces three pieces of parchment and hands one to each of us. 'You will need these, to wrap up your prize.'

I glance at the page. At the top it says *Adonais by Percy Bysshe Shelley*. Even with this clue, my numb and sluggish brain doesn't realise what is coming. I kneel with the others – it seems the right thing to do – and as my knees touch the paving and my fingers touch the stone jar I feel some nameless ancient dread. With as much trepidation as if I am turning the handle of a jack-in-the-box, I open the lid. A metallic odour emanates from within, reminiscent of a butcher shop. Reaching into that black void is one of the most nerve-wracking things I've done in my life. At every moment I expect unseen teeth to fasten on my flesh. My tingling fingers meet something solid and slimy, a something that shifts when I try to hold it. I find some purchase and draw the thing out, and it makes a dreadful sucking sound as it comes free from the jar. I look at what lies in my hands, but I need no instruction from Ulysses about what it is. I know well enough from this week's biology lesson. This is a heart, disembodied, squat and stinking, the vessels leaking blood that looks black in the moonlight. I nearly drop mine. Jess cries out at the sight of his, and Calvin vomits abruptly on his shoes. Somewhere in the graveyard sounds the unearthly shriek of a nocturnal animal meeting its end in the jaws of some predator.

Ulysses speaks again. 'For the coming days, from now until the Feathers Ball on Saturday, you must carry your heart with you everywhere you go. You must wrap the heart in the Shelley poem *Adonais*, just as Mary did. You must no more leave your new heart at home than you would your own heart. When I say everywhere, I mean *everywhere*. Now, gentlemen, let's to bed.'

The Squabs follow The Gothic Boys out of the cemetery, carrying our grisly trophies. I know intellectually that the hearts must indeed be from the butcher shop, the offal of some hapless sheep or pig. But for that short walk back to New Haven School, I can't escape the thought that the heavy organ in my hands is human. The blood soaks through the poem into my skin and the paper whispers like a curse.

I wake up in the morning to an odd lump in my pillow and a decaying smell.

I'd shoved the heart under my pillow last night. The one thing I'd learned about The Gloomth is to take what they say literally. If they said to *keep the heart with you at all times*, then they mean keep the heart with you at all times. I draw the package out. The gore has soaked through the paper and on to the sheets, but I don't worry about this too much – the bedding at New Haven is changed every day, like a hotel. This could easily be a nosebleed.

I notice the poem is almost entirely red – but one line stands out pale on the page like a scar.

'. . . the ever-beating heart
Shook the white hand that grasped it . . .'

My hands shake too as I stuff the thing into the drawstring shoe bag that came with my new school shoes. I've got time before homeroom, so I set off for town.

The Stop 'n' Shop in New Haven, which seems to be open twenty-four-seven, is already teeming with customers. In the back they stock everything from doormats to toilet plungers to umbrellas, so I'm hopeful they'll have what I'm looking for. I scan the shelves and my eyes light on just what I need. A fanny pack, which clips round the waist with a belt – tough and many zipped. Just right for carrying a phone or a wallet or your keys.

Or a disembodied heart.

I pick black and move on to the kitchen section. I select a roll of plastic storage bags, and take both goods to the counter. The teller smiles brightly at me. She wouldn't smile like that if she knew what the bags were for.

Outside the store I take out the bloody parcel. The shoe bag is slick with blood on the inside so I put it in a nearby trash can. I pop the poem-wrapped heart in a baggie, sealing the top, then put the whole thing in the fanny pack. I clip the bag around my waist under my uniform, adjusting the belt so it's nice and high, round my waist not my hips. It gives me a bit of a gut but that's well hidden by the blousing of my shirt and the fall of my blazer. I straighten up and look at myself in the window of the Stop 'n' Shop. I don't look like a fellow who is concealing body parts about his person. Good. Now I'm ready to face my day.

As it turns out, I was absolutely right to take The Gloomth literally. Over the coming days, one of the four Gothic Boys will do periodic spot checks to make sure the heart is with me – in class, at dinner, in the boat, on the river. Iggy even wakes me in the night once, and I'm forced to pull back the bedclothes to show him the fanny pack around my waist. I've taken to sleeping on my back while my fleshy friend is with me. I sometimes think that the rotting heart is beating, like the Tell-Tale Heart that ticked beneath the floorboards and gave away a murderer. I have the oddest feeling that this organ, what Shelley called *the ever-beating heart*, will give me away to The Gloomth – a visceral witness giving damning testament as to who I am and why I'm here.

On the Friday, the eve of the Feathers Ball, I realise that the plastic bag has inflated. The bacteria have done their work, and the heart has cooked itself into a festering fist. I open the bag and it puffs forth a foul odour such as I have never smelled before. Trying not to hurl, I take the heart out. The thing stinks and the poem is mush, but I hesitate to throw the shredded verses away – for all I know they could be part of the pledge. Instead, I dry the thing off with paper towels and replace it in the fanny pack without the plastic bag. That last day before the Feathers Ball the heart literally hardens. It blackens and becomes rigid, the vessels drying and closing, just like my own. I no longer feel like the heart is beating. *I weep for Adonais – he is dead*, I think. Now I feel safe – the heart can't give me away.

The other Squabs are not so lucky. Still not quite grasping that to pledge for The Gloomth means letting go of logic entirely, on that final day they both get caught out in different, and equally brutal ways.

We are doing cross-country when Jess messes up. Halfway through the school park, well out of sight of Coach Rubens, the Gothic Boys stop us for a spot check. I have my black heart in the fanny pack, and Calvin, ingeniously, has his in a cool bag in a little backpack on his back, nestling, disgustingly, next to his water. But Jess is found wanting. 'Here too?' he says. 'Are you serious?'

'Deadly,' says Lowell. In one of those bewildering looks that The Gloomth seems to specialise in, there are no smiling faces or joshing elbows, as there were on the run just five minutes before. The Gothic Boys are as serious as the grave.

'It's in the locker room,' Jess pleads. 'I never thought . . .'

'No,' says Iggy. 'You never did. Go get it.'

'Now?'

'Yes,' says Oliver. 'Now.'

'But it's m . . . miles.'

'Then you'd better get going,' says Ulysses. 'We'll wait.'

Jess has to run all the way back to school and get the heart. The rest of us wait. When Jess arrives, red in the face and clutching his gym bag, he looks like he's been crying. He's breathing so fast I think he's going to pass out. I've learned my lesson from the night of the Green Fairy and I don't object. Jess throws up twice from the exertion and my own heart blackens against the Gothic Boys.

Back at the school it's Calvin's turn. A jock to his bones, he doesn't attempt to dodge the showers like any normal person, but always rushes into the communal block and douses himself straight away, as joyous as an otter. Today I follow, still wearing my fanny pack and nothing else, and the exhausted Jess, noting what I've done, takes his gym bag, with the air of one who'll never set it down again. But it's too late to warn Calvin. He's already soaping himself vigorously when The Gloomth catch up with him. Naked, they surround him.

'Where's your heart?' asks Ulysses above the pounding of the water, his dark hair plastered to his head, cheekbones even more stark, long lashes as spiky as spiders' legs.

Calvin stops, soapy hands together as if in prayer. 'What, here too? You gotta be kidding me.'

'I kid you not,' says Ulysses. 'Where did you leave it?'

'Just by the outside door,' says Calvin. 'I didn't want to bring it into the locker room. It's kinda . . . funky.'

'Go get it,' commands Lowell.

'But it's cold.'

'Then go quickly,' says Iggy.

Calvin looks at them, from one stony, beautiful face to the next. For one moment they stand there, in suspended animation, like Greek statues in the rain. Then, without another word, Calvin leaves the shower and goes back into the locker room.

In a moment he's back. 'Coach took it to lost and found,' he says. 'He thought another class left it.'

'Then go get it,' says Ulysses.

'But lost and found is all the way over in the main building,' Calvin whines. 'I'll have to cross the sports field.'

'Yes,' says Lowell. 'You will.'

'But it's zero degrees out,' protests Calvin. 'Have a heart.' He obviously hears it a moment after he says it.

'If you had a heart,' says Iggy triumphantly, 'you wouldn't need to go fetch it. Now, march.'

Calvin, resigned, reaches for his towel. Oliver gets there first.

'No towel,' he says, clenching the material in a bony hand. He throws the towel on the floor of the shower, where it instantly darkens and soaks. It's such a dick move I could have hit him right then and there. Calvin's jaw clenches, the muscle bunching and dimpling, and I can see he feels the same, but he knows better by now than to protest. He exits the shower, dripping, and walks naked through the ranks of astonished boys in the locker room, leaving a trail of footprints. The Gothic Boys grab their towels and wrap them around their waists, climbing on the wooden bench to peer out the high windows. This is barbaric. But I sling my own towel around my waist and join the rest of them, rubbernecking at Calvin's humiliation. A whole bunch of eighth graders are playing football, and stop to stare, giggling incredulously at the sight of Calvin, buck naked and shivering, running barefoot the length of the field. His humiliation is complete. I feel rage fill me up and overflow.

A trickle travels the length of my leg and I look down. The shower has soaked my fanny pack and the heart has rehydrated, reanimated. A stream of blood runs down my leg and through the slats in the bench to pool in the drain.

When the three of us Squabs go up to the dormitory that night, equally vanquished in our own separate ways, we all find a single pigeon feather on our pillows. The other two are so attuned to misfortune by now that they look at each other and then at me with dread.

'What now?' asks Jess in a voice weary with fear, twirling the pigeon feather in front of his face.

'No,' I say. 'It's all right. It's just an invitation.'

'To what?' asks Jess.

'To the Feathers Ball,' I say. 'It's tomorrow. Remember? *They* talked about it at the Egyptian Gate.'

There's no need to elaborate on who 'they' are.

'Not much of an invitation,' says Calvin. 'It doesn't tell you where or when.'

'They don't tell you,' I say, 'because you're supposed to know.'

And of course, I do know. I've been prepared for this, rehearsed, tutored. And now I can't wait. My spirits soar abruptly. Because whatever else tomorrow night may bring, I know at least I will see Harper again.

# PART 5

## Porphyria's Lover

'And thus we sit together now,
And all night long we have not stirred,
And yet God has not said a word.'
    *Porphyria's Lover* – Robert Browning, 1836

# 1

I hadn't realised how much I missed Harper, missed having a friend to talk to. A friend who knows everything – well, nearly everything. Someone who interacts normally, without wanting to draw you in, psych you out, belittle you. This evening I'll be seeing the other Ida Barney girls too – Stevie, Reuter and the enigmatic Anna. As someone who had, once in another life, a mother figure who loved me so much, I realise that I miss the society of women, the people who seem to care about me, even if I am just a way to fatten their CVs and boost their Ivy League applications. And there is another reason I am anxious to see Harper. I want to ask her about the kiss with Ulysses on the ice the day Timmie died. Why had she edited the story for me? And does she still have feelings for Ulysses Parslow?

As I get ready for the Feathers Ball, jostling for showers and mirrors with the rest of my dorm, I feel oddly nervous. I tuck the feather invitation into my top pocket, so that it protrudes like a pocket square. I remember seeing this detail on the CCTV footage of last year. My hands shake as I fasten the pigeon skull pin at my throat, so much so that I have to take a breath and start again. The last thing I need is to prick my finger and bleed all over my white cravat. By tonight, if all goes well, there will be a tiny camera inside that silver cranium, and I find the thought immensely comforting – for the next pledge, whatever it is, I won't be alone. Harper will scarcely believe what I have to tell her about the night of the Green Fairy, the Squab dinner and the heart challenge.

I take one last look in the mirror, and as a finishing touch I pull the golden Van Buren medallion outside of my shirt to hang below my cravat. Now I am the very image of the Brat in the CCTV footage I saw from the Feathers Ball last year – curls smooth, cheeks shaven, Gloomth uniform immaculate, pigeon beak pointing determinedly to the left. But it is an illusion. We may look the same, but everything else is different.

I head downstairs with the rest of the seniors. Along with The Gloomth, only the twelfth graders are invited, with the equivalent cohort from Ida Barney, and the juniors must occupy themselves quietly in their respective schoolhouses. First, we go into the grounds, where there is a reception.

The gardens are a dreamland. The hedges have been clipped to resemble birds, and adorned with fairy lights. Great paper bird-shaped kites bend and swoop on pliable poles thrust into the grass. Torches line the yew walks, their flames marking the way and reminding me uncomfortably of the dark labyrinth beneath the chapel. A white marquee rises from the lawn like an iceberg, and inside are waiters dressed in snowy livery with a feather on each lapel. They form a plain canvas for the bevy of beauties who await us. Our counterparts are a riot of colour like an aviary of brightly plumed birds themselves. Stainless-steel heaters belch out enough heat to keep them warm in their silks and satins, but for the moment I can't see any of the reporters from *The Star*, and I suddenly feel incredibly shy in this sea of oestrogen. There are enormous punch bowls hung about with silver ladles. For something to do, I pour myself a cup and take a drink. It's basically soda. A voice at my elbow says, 'Yes, please.'

It's Harper, and she looks dazzling tonight. She is dressed in a gown reminiscent of a flapper dress of the 1920s, made of overlapping feathers the same pale gold as her hair. The look is completed by long necklace of moon-pale pearls. She looks like a gilded idol.

'Hey, Scoop,' I say, trying to play it cool in the face of her beauty. I take up the ladle again. 'It's non-alcoholic, of course,' I say.

'That won't last long,' she says. 'Look.'

She points across the bar to where Oliver and Iggy, creased up with laughter at their own ingenuity, are covertly pouring a quart bottle of Tito's into the vast bowl. 'Give it a minute,' she says. 'Let's wait for the vodka to hit.'

I smile. I lay my cup aside, stir the mixture with the ladle, then pour two more. We clink and drink. Thanks to the vodka, the punch now has quite a kick. 'How are you?'

'Fine,' she says. 'More to the point, how are *you*?'

'I've got a lot to tell you,' I murmur.

'I should think so,' she says, raising her voice so Iggy and Oliver can hear. 'Taking off on vacation for a whole year without so much as a word. I ought to throw this punch right in your face.'

'Well, I hope you won't do that.'

I get the message. I'm supposed to be Brat, and this is supposed to be the first time she's seen me in a year. 'You look lovely by the way,' I say. 'I should have opened with that.'

'Yes, I do. And yes, you should have.'

I offer her my arm, the epitome of chivalry. 'Now we have our drinks, shall we go explore?'

We follow the crowd to the school. At the doorway is an immense feather arch, like a giant boa, with foil letters proclaiming: BIRDS OF A FEATHER STICK TOGETHER. An apt comment on Connecticut society. I look up at the CCTV cameras – this shot must be a carbon copy of the tape from last year – Brat and Harper walking under the archway of feathers.

When we enter the Great Hall, the place is transformed. I have no idea when the decorations committee had a chance to do all this stuff, since at noon this place looked like a regular lunchroom, but now there are silver tapestries on the walls depicting all manner of birds, from the humble pigeon (of course) to his more tropical cousins. Swathes of delicate material sewn with a million crystals drape the windows, and, most impressive of all, what looks like a thousand silver feathers hang from the ceiling at different heights, dangling on filaments so thin they look like they are suspended unaided. There is not a sit-down dinner, like the one at Ida Barney where I met Harper, but rather a long trestle table piled high with a luscious buffet. My stomach does a backflip – I'm too on edge about getting caught to make myself a plate. But a gentleman has to look after his date, so I ask Harper, 'Are you hungry?'

'Not in the least. Let's dance. Then we can talk.'

The stage at the far end of the hall, which is usually used for speech days and school plays, is crammed with a band complete with a full brass section. The band's name is emblazoned on the bass drum – The Black Birds. No DJs at New Haven, clearly. The musicians are cycling through the most toe-tapping swing playlist, in the face of which it is hard to keep still. As they strike up 'Rockin' Robin', we give in to it and take to the floor.

As soon as we are safe on an island of music, surrounded by a sea of couples, we dance cheek to cheek and Harper talks into my ear. 'How's it been going? Your GPS didn't really tell us anything. All around the school grounds except for a night in Grove End Cemetery. That about right?'

'Well, that doesn't really tell the whole story,' I say. And over the next three songs, I fill in the detail, about *The Castle of Otranto* and the Green Fairy, the Squab dinner and the Exchange of the Tears and the jars and Shelley's heart. She is surprised and disgusted in turn, and when I've finished she doesn't say anything for quite a while, and we just dance, while she lets it all sink in.

'Have you noticed what they are doing?'

'Who, The Gloomth?'

'No,' she says. 'The band. They are playing all bird songs with bird titles. "Rockin' Robin". "Bye Bye Blackbird".'

'Clever,' I say. 'So on brand.'

'The problem we have now,' she says, 'is that I don't know what comes next. Brat only told me about *The Castle of Otranto* pledge. Nothing about the Squab dinner or Shelley's heart challenge.'

'He wasn't even supposed to tell you that,' I say. 'Before the first pledge you sign in blood to keep it secret. He must have really liked you.'

She doesn't respond to that. 'Well, look. The first pledge is to do with *The Castle of Otranto*, the first Gothic novel. The second is related to Mary Shelley and *Frankenstein*, arguably the greatest ever Gothic novel, and the first by a woman. Like I said, I got the feeling from Brat that the keys to *all* of the pledges you'll be asked to do will be found in Gothic literature. Just keep everything you've read in mind, and the answers should be there.'

'For each pledge Lewis Walpole taught a particular text in class that day,' I say. '*The Castle of Otranto* for the Green Fairy challenge, and *Frankenstein* for Shelley's heart challenge.'

'There you go,' she says. 'Whatever he teaches next, you can bet a dime to a dollar that's going to be your next pledge. My God,' she says, eyes shining, 'this is great stuff. It's going to make an amazing article.' Again, I get the uncomfortable feeling that the spark in her eyes is to do with the story, not me.

I draw Harper closer. There's something I want to ask her, about the night of the Exchange of the Tears.

'Ulysses told me.'

She draws back and looks at me, eyes wide with shock.

'About the night that Timmie died. He said that you kissed. That you were kissing when she fell through the ice.' Something flits across her face. Is it relief? 'Why didn't you tell me?'

'I don't know,' she says. 'I honestly don't know. I mean, partly guilt. I do sometimes feel like if he hadn't been kissing me, Timmie might still be alive. But I didn't even know Timmie was still out on the ice, I swear I didn't. I thought when I took Stellan back Uly would have taken Timmie home too – it was kind of cold for the little ones.' I register the nickname, the intimacy of it, with the force of a blow. 'And then when he came over to me on the lake, he was on his own. Then it just kind of happened. It was my first kiss with Uly. My first kiss ever, actually.'

'Was it your *last* kiss with him?'

'If you're asking me if it happened again, no,' she says. 'How could it after that? And I told you, he changed. Completely. And then I met Brat. You. I met you. And then I changed too.'

I want to believe her. She is so shining and beautiful and as we sway to the music I begin to feel a bit drunk – not just on Iggy's vodka. But for the first time I get the idea that, like the Green Fairy, she is not entirely well intentioned. Why is she doing this? Out of a philanthropic desire to help me take down The Gloomth? To round out her college applications? Or because she really fell in love with Brat last fall?'

'What are you thinking?' she says.

'That you could be a Mercedes,' I say, unguarded.

'Why would I be a car?' she asks.

I laugh, and it breaks the moment open like a bird's egg. Maybe it's the music, or the beauty, or the vodka, but I decide to take a risk.

'Have you heard of a book called *The Count of Monte Cristo*?'

'I've heard of it, but I've never read it.'

Good. I'm safe.

'Is it a Gothic novel?'

'I think so,' I say. 'In fact, to all accounts I had a spirited argument with Lewis Walpole about that very question last fall. When he is young, the count falls in love with a beautiful young girl called Mercedes. They are engaged to be married and pledge to be together forever. Then he's imprisoned for years on a remote island, for a crime he didn't commit, and everyone thinks he's dead. When he returns, he finds that Mercedes is married to his deadliest enemy.'

'What's that got to do with me?'

'Well, it was you who told me all about the Parslows and the Van Burens and their feud. I'm just wondering how Brat would feel about you being in the arms of the enemy.'

'How would *you* feel,' she corrects me. 'You are Brat, remember? How *would* you feel?'

'Jealous,' I say. 'Vengeful. Dangerous.'

She leans in, just as Ulysses had done on the night he drank my tears. 'You're forgetting something,' she murmurs in my ear. 'I was never yours to begin with. *Eddie.*' The whisper is as soft as a breath, so no one can hear it but me. She draws back, eyes enormous, challenging. Our mouths are very close together and I can feel a tingling heat, like electricity jumping a gap. I bend towards her, as if compelled.

Just then I feel a tap on my shoulder.

It's enormously frustrating to be interrupted at that moment. I turn, fists and teeth clenched, to see Ulysses Parslow standing there.

He looks like Poe dressed in Prada. All cheekbones, hollow eyes and flopping dark hair. The silver pigeon skull at his throat dimmed by the silver of his eyes.

'Harper,' he says, lifting her hand and kissing it. 'The belle of the ball as ever.'

'Hello, Uly,' she says, all politeness. 'It's been a minute.'

He devours her with his eyes. 'Mind if I cut in?' he asks me, without taking his eyes off Harper.

I do mind. I mind so much that for a moment I can't speak.

'You can't hog her all night, you know,' Ulysses says, all charm. 'Give the other fellows a chance.'

I back away. Maybe it is a good idea for Harper to dance with Ulysses. With the sheer wattage of her beauty tonight and her journalistic habit of interrogation, she might be able to worm something out of him. And I certainly need to find Anna. After the double fright of the last two pledges, I want to be fitted with that camera as soon as possible.

I thread my way through the crowd in search of Anna. On my way, I see Reuter, who is dressed in an orange gown that clashes gloriously with her red hair, and Stevie, who looks magnificent in a tuxedo with her hair slicked back. Of course, I'm not supposed to know them, so I glide by and pause, looking like I'm engaging in some small talk, and say, out of the side of my mouth, 'Is Anna around?'

'She's at the buffet,' says Stevie.

'You can usually find her wherever there's food,' smiles Reuter.

I walk over to the buffet table.

'Hey,' I say. She puts the plate down and turns round, almost as if she's been caught stealing. And then I see the full glory of her. She's in a long dress made of embroidered red silk. Her sheet of black hair falls dead straight almost to her waist, held back by a red hairband with a long red tassel at each temple, which hang like earrings. Her eyes are accentuated with a sweep of black eyeliner and her lips are ruby red. She looks entirely different from the geek girl in uniform who I met at Ida Barney. She's still unsmiling, and her gaze is disquietingly direct. But she looks a million dollars.

'Good,' she says. 'Let's get this over with.'

She grabs my hand in a surprisingly strong grip and drags me to the dance floor. At first, we dance in hold but quite far apart. She looks over my shoulder, and I get the feeling she's waiting an exact number of songs before she takes me outside. She seems entirely unbothered by the silence but I can't take it. I say the first thing I can think of. 'Where are your feathers?'

She looks at me witheringly. 'I'm literally covered in cranes,' she says.

I look more closely at her dress. It's embroidered with little golden cranes in gilt thread, and they also fly around the neckline, sleeves and hem. 'In Japanese culture, cranes symbolise good luck, longevity, peace and fidelity.'

I'm taken aback. 'Harper said you were Chinese,' I say.

'Harper doesn't know.'

By the third song, the band slow it down and strike up a melody that is all too familiar to me. It is 'Blackbird', by the Beatles. Memory douses me like a bucket of cold water, and just for a few seconds I can neither move nor talk.

Anna becomes aware that she is suddenly dancing with a block of wood. 'This song means a lot to you, huh?'

Wordless, I nod.

'Harper never told me much. About who you are, I mean.'

I repeat her own comment. 'Harper doesn't know.' Then it strikes me that Harper's never asked me a single thing about my life – about me as Eddie, that is. Apart from the few details she needed for her contract, she never showed any curiosity about my hard-luck story. I take a shaky breath. 'I'm an orphan, a ward of the state and I was working in a diner when Harper met me. This song was my favourite when I was little. Because it was the favourite of a . . . woman who loved me.'

'What happened to her?'

'She died.'

'Life's been tough for you.' It's a statement of fact. For the first time her voice seems to have no edges; it is rounded, soft, sympathetic.

'It nearly killed me.'

She pulls me close and jams her cheek to mine. It might be just for the benefit of the Gothic Boys, but it is the nearest thing I've had to a hug for a long, long time. Then she murmurs, 'I understand. I'm not one of them either.'

I listen intently above the music. 'I'm a scholarship girl,' she says. 'We have no money. My parents moved from Japan ten years ago. We have a restaurant in New Haven. I've worked there since I was thirteen. When I first went to Ida Barney the girls used to tease me, saying I smelled of fish sauce.'

'Even Harper?'

'Especially Harper. Look.' She breathes in and out again, like she's preparing a speech. 'In Japan, they do this thing where if you break a vase, you stick it together again, but you use gold. It's called kintsugi.' She lets me go so she can look in my eyes. 'You can still see the cracks, but the vase is even more beautiful than it was before. Just because you're broken, doesn't mean you can't be beautiful.' She still doesn't smile, but it is one of the kindest things that anyone's ever said to me. It almost brings me to tears. The song ends just before they can fall, and Anna takes my hand again. '*Now* we can go,' she says.

We slip like shadows out into the night. It's cold outside, and it's even colder outside of Anna's embrace. There's a little summer house by the lake – now very much a winter house. I go to give Anna my jacket, just like I wanted to do for Harper at the Commencement Dinner, but she stops me. 'Don't do that chivalry bullshit,' she says. 'I'm fine. Let's get to it.'

She snaps open her tiny ruby-encrusted bag and takes out a little black box with rounded corners. It's the size of a ring box, and it feels for one moment like I'm on the receiving end of a proposal. That is, until she opens the box and it turns into the weirdest proposal ever. In a little sponge housing lies a little black sphere with a lens. It's wreathed by a tiny black wire with a charging port. 'This,' says Anna, as if she's describing a fifty-carat diamond, 'is a 1080P Mini Wi-Fi Camera. It has wireless surveillance security with night vision, motion detection and 160-degree audio recording.'

'I don't know what any of that means.'

'How often do you wear it?' she asks. 'The pigeon skull, I mean?'

'Just at Gloomth meetings, and events like this.'

'So you wear it for every pledge?'

'Yes. Them's the rules.'

'OK, great,' she says. 'This is the charger. You can plug it into a laptop or a regular phone adaptor. Make sure it's fully charged before each Gloomth event. There's a tiny green power light *here*.' She shows me. 'Green fully charged; red dead.'

'Green charged; red dead,' I parrot. 'Got it.'

She pops the camera through the eye socket of the silver skull, where it sits securely.

'It fits perfectly,' I say admiringly.

'I checked it with a real pigeon's skull,' she says matter-of-factly.

'Wow. You really go all-out when you have a project, don't you?'

'Let's not start handing out Nobel Prizes just yet,' she says. 'We don't know if it works.'

She gets her phone out of her bag, wakes it up and hands it to me. 'Watch this as I turn around 360 degrees,' she says. 'I have to calibrate it.' She holds the skull in her fingers and turns round and round on the wooden platform of the summer house like she's a ballerina in one of those music boxes little girls have.

I watch the phone screen as I'm bid, and as she turns I can see a pin-sharp picture of the lake, the summer house and finally my own image as she faces my way. 'Cool,' she says, sitting down next to me. 'We're live. Let me pin it back on you.'

She reaches up to my throat.

'No,' I say. 'Beak to the left.' I turn the little silver cranium, our fingers meet, our eyes do too and suddenly we're holding hands. A twig snaps in the undergrowth and I see Anna's eyes widen. Then, suddenly, she presses her ruby mouth on mine, in a passionate kiss.

Suddenly I'm alight, the cold forgotten, and I kiss her back with the fervour of a starving man who's just found food, my hands in the warmth of her silken hair. Then I hear jeering and cheering, catcalling and whooping, and we break apart and look up.

The Gothic Boys stand before us with Ulysses at their centre. Iggy, Oliver and Lowell are applauding. Ulysses looks stern, but also somehow relieved. And I'm ninety per cent sure it's because he's seen me kissing a girl who isn't Harper. His eyes travel down to my open collar, top button undone.

'Where's your pigeon skull?'

Anna opens her hand to show a flash of silver. 'My bad,' she says. 'We were getting a little hot and heavy, you know? I was trying to undo his shirt, so I took this bird thing off.'

I smile and shrug, channelling my best douchebag *'she's only human'* look.

Ulysses considers this. 'I won't admonish you in front of a lady,' he says to me. 'So I'll let this one go. But I will just remind you that this is a Gloomth event – the fraternity are hosting this ball for the school. Therefore you are required to wear full Gloomth uniform at all times.'

'Sorry,' I say. I take the skull from Anna and refasten it, beak to the left. I hope against hope that Ulysses can't see that tiny pinprick of the green power light.

'We'll leave you to your amorous endeavours,' he says, possibly the most Ulysses Parslow utterance ever. 'But, Brat. The skull stays *on*. Remember that.'

'Oh, don't worry,' I say. 'I will.'

As they walk away I let out a shaky breath and wait a moment before I speak. 'That was quick thinking,' I say, smiling at her. 'Thank you.'

'No problem,' she says, all back to business. She still doesn't smile. I wonder, not for the first time, if she ever does. I feel light-headed, drunk, and it's nothing to do with Iggy's vodka. I'm drunk on her kiss.

Anna follows Ulysses Parslow with her eyes as he walks away along the torchlit paths, back ramrod straight, hands in pockets. 'Straight back to tell Harper,' she notes.

'You think?' The notion doesn't hurt as much as it might have a quarter-hour earlier.

'Oh, one hundred per cent,' she says. 'Anything to win her back. Did you manage to do the debrief?'

'Yes,' I say. 'While we were dancing. I get the feeling Harper was already scribbling in her head.'

'No need,' she says. 'I set her up with a dictaphone. She'll have recorded everything you said.' She looks at me sideways. 'She didn't tell you?'

'No,' I say grimly. 'She didn't.'

A small silence falls, neither one of us wanting to criticise Harper out loud. But was that a bit of a snaky thing to do? Aren't journalists supposed to tell you when you're on the record? Was I a source or a friend? And was that a dance or an interview?

Anna jerks her head towards the school. 'I'd better get back.'

'Sure,' I say, collecting myself. I stand when she stands, unable, quite yet, to let go of what she calls *the chivalry bullshit*. 'I'll see you around,' I say.

'I'll certainly see *you*,' she says. 'Well, I won't see you, but I'll see what you see.'

I let her get ahead and then wander back. My steps are leisurely, but my feelings are agitated. What happened here tonight? That kiss shattered my world, turned me upside down. Suddenly I need to see her again, to ask her if it was real. I return to the Great Hall, and my eyes search the room. I see Harper dancing once again with Ulysses. But this time I don't even care that she is in the arms of the enemy. Something has changed. My eyes travel past her and search the crowd for a figure in red. My eyes light on Anna, and white spots seems to dance before my eyes. I would think it had started to snow, except for the fact that I'm inside. I look up: feathers are falling from an enormous release net that is high in the cross ribs. Everyone looks up and starts smiling and clapping with delight – and in the middle of them all is Anna in her red silk, spinning round and round, arms out-flung to catch the feathers, laughing and laughing.

It is a relatively quiet rest of the weekend – a little too quiet, like the calm before the storm.

I spend my free time on tenterhooks, once again waiting for the other shoe to drop. And on Monday, it does. First thing is literature class with Lewis Walpole, and, recalling my conversation with Harper, I know that whatever we study next will indicate the nature of the next pledge to join The Gloomth.

It all starts so innocently. Lewis Walpole, betweeded as usual, strides over to the board and writes, in his sweeping hand, *Porphyria'ſ Lover*. My brain does that automatic thing it does now when confronted with Gloomth script, which is to convert the F to an S in my mind. I remember abruptly that of course Lewis Walpole was one of the original Gloomth members, so he would have been one of the cohort that originated this way of writing. I recognise what he's actually written, which is PORPHYRIA'S LOVER.

'Got a treat for you today, boys,' he says. '*Porphyria's Lover*. A little Gothic gem by a master of the genre.'

Below the title he writes the name of the author, as he always does:

## *ROBERT BROWNING*

'*Porphyria's Lover,*' he says. 'By Robert Browning. A poet with a taste for the Gothic-grotesque. Just like you fellows. Let's give it a read.'

As ever, the class read the poem in turn. To begin with, as Iggy begins to read, the poem seems to have nothing to do with the Gothic at all – sure, it is set on a dark and stormy night, but the poet meets his lover, Porphyria, in secret in a cottage by a lake for a midnight tryst. Everything goes swimmingly, and Oliver reads the part where their love seems to be at its height and the poet realises how Porphyria worships him and how much he adores her.

But then, as Ulysses takes over, things get very dark indeed:

> *That moment she was mine, mine, fair,*
> *Perfectly pure and good: I found*
> *A thing to do, and all her hair*
> *In one long yellow string I wound*
> *Three times her little throat around,*
> *And strangled her. No pain felt she;*
> *I am quite sure she felt no pain.*

Wow. It falls to me to read the final stanza, when things get even darker:

> *I propped her head up as before,*
> > *Only, this time my shoulder bore*
> *Her head, which droops upon it still:*
> > *The smiling rosy little head,*
> *So glad it has its utmost will,*
> > *That all it scorned at once is fled,*
> > *And I, its love, am gained instead!*
> *Porphyria's love: she guessed not how*
> > *Her darling one wish would be heard.*
> *And thus we sit together now,*
> > *And all night long we have not stirred,*
> > *And yet God has not said a word!*

'What's the message of the poem?' asks the professor.

Basically, a guy kills his lover then he sits up all night embracing her corpse. But that's not what Lewis Walpole wants to hear. In his class you have to come up with something a bit more erudite than that.

'Mr Emerson?'

Jess wakes up. 'It's about obsessive love turning into murder.'

'Yes,' says Professor Walpole. 'What else?'

'It's about worship. Porphyria worships her lover, and he wants to keep her adoration for eternity.'

'That too,' he says. 'Anything else?

There's a short silence. Then Ulysses speaks, in his refined New England accent. 'It's about control.'

Lewis Walpole points his chalk at him, his usual accolade if someone says something right. '*Yes*,' he says. 'How so?'

'Well,' drawls Ulysses, 'when Porphyria is alive, he waits for the height of her passion, the zenith of her feelings for him. And *that's* when he decides she must die. Then she can never change, she can never betray him. She will always be a golden goddess to him.'

*A golden goddess.* That's what I thought about Harper on the night of the Feathers Ball. I must have made some involuntary movement, some little sound, because Lewis Walpole turns to me like a hawk hearing a mouse.

'Mr Van Buren. Anything to add?'

'Yes,' I say. 'He'd rather have a dead goddess than a live woman.'

The professor puts his head on one side, eyes twinkling. 'Why?'

I lean back in my chair. 'Because girls are real,' I say. 'They might have a blemish. They might be cranky. They might not smile when you want them to. They might not say what you want them to say, do what you want them to do. They might love you one day, not love you the next. They might even fall in love with someone else. If you are *really* in love with someone, you would love them anyway, flaws and all. But if you are a dangerous, thin-skinned narcissist psychopath' – here I look pointedly at Ulysses – 'you might decide that a woman is better dead with you, than alive without you. The poet killed Porphyria when she was at her most perfect, her most golden, her most devoted. And he made sure she would never change. I would say it's about possession as well as control.'

'You're both right,' the professor says. 'Good, both of you. Possession. Control. Two of the most dangerous words in the English language.'

For the rest of the day I'm back on tenterhooks, wondering what is coming next.

If The Gloomth are indeed capable of murder, and the only blonde around is Harper, does that mean she is in danger? A cold tide of foreboding washes over me. Did she give something away to Ulysses while in his arms at the Feathers Ball? Did she betray that she knew too much about The Gloomth? Or that she was planning to write an exposé on them? I can't fight the growing feeling that it is Ulysses Parslow's mission to possess Harper, to make his childhood sweetheart his adulthood sweetheart, and that's why he had to remove the threat of Brat. And I'm beginning to get the even more uncomfortable feeling that possession would count for him even if she was dead.

It's bedtime when we three Squabs discover our fate. Each one of us finds a parchment on our beds in the dormitory, speared to the pillow with a pigeon feather. The other boys are bedding down, chatting and fooling about. Jess looks at Calvin and me.

'Let's take these downstairs,' he says.

We sneak down the back stairs to the cloister, and Calvin produces a lighter from somewhere and holds it high while I unfurl my letter. There is the same handwriting, the same Ss masquerading as Fs, that single elongated letter now invested with the power to terrify. Butts on the cold stone, we read of our task, with the same age-old weariness of Hercules wondering what the hell kind of labour he has to do next.

*Bartholomew Van Buren III*

*In the spirit of Robert Browning's Porphyria's Lover, you are charged to spend the night in the mortuary of Yale Medical school. You must spend the entire night there, until dawn, without discovery. This is the first of three Cardinal challenges, which are elimination stages. Failure of any squab to complete this challenge will result in an unsuccessful pledge.*

Then at the bottom of the letter, ten words, underlined for emphasis.

*<u>This is not a group challenge. You must go alone.</u>*

We look at each other, in the moonlight, wide of eye and pale of cheek. To spend time alone with the dead. To be the only living soul in a crowded room is a thing almost too terrible to contemplate. But, terrifying as the prospect is, I've made a decision, one which makes my heart race and my stomach lurch.

I'm going to go *tonight*.

My thinking is that if we've all got to go on our own, then the person who goes first has the best chance of success. If one of us fails and is found out, then security will be increased and it will be much harder for the ones who come after. And I may not know what pledges lie ahead but I know one thing, and that is that it's absolutely essential that I get through to the final challenge. The whole plan, exposé, sting, whatever this is, depends on that.

Calvin peers at the letter. 'How do we even get into Yale Med?' he asks. 'We can't exactly just walk in.'

'There's gotta be a way,' says Jess. 'But the trick is how to go undetected.'

I look at them, marvelling that they would even want to carry on pledging faced with such a task. I mean, I know why *I'm* doing this, but it's quite something to be ready to commit such an act against the law, and, moreover, against common decency.

But then I try to see what's on offer from the point of view of someone who wasn't born into all this stuff. What The Gloomth are offering are not just a few opera tickets and a good berth for your yacht in the Hamptons. Membership of The Gloomth means you're set for life. There's nothing that creates a greater bond than a dark secret. I should know. And that's why members go straight to the best Ivy League schools. Then they graduate *summa cum laude*, breeze into Fortune 500 jobs and are guaranteed a place on the board, in the Senate, in Congress. Even in the White House. And I suppose it *is* a selection process of sorts, since only the fittest get through the challenges. I look at Calvin and Jess. Granted, they don't have my foreknowledge, but they still seem to take a little time catching on. If this *is* survival of the fittest, maybe Darwinism is going to be on my side.

So instead of saying: *We know how to get to Yale Med. They literally showed us. Theophilus Eaton's tomb, remember? The steam tunnels that go all the way to Yale?* I just say, instead: 'That, as Hamlet said, is the question.'

We cross the dark cloister and climb the staircase back to the dormitory, but I don't go to bed.

Silently, stealthily, I dress in my Gloomth uniform. The dorm is configured so your bed and closet give you a small corner of privacy – enough to dress beyond the gaze of others.

I'm mindful of the rule laid down by the Committee of Taste, to look immaculate at every pledge. Before I button the shirt, though, I have a sudden thought. I go to my closet and take out my thick New Haven letterman soccer sweater. I pull it on and replace the shirt on top. A bit bulky, but you'd never tell. The one thing I know about morgues is that they are supposed to be cold, so it's better to be prepared for the long hours ahead.

Once I'm fully suited, I pick up the little pigeon skull from my bedside table. Triggered by movement, the tiny green light of the camera kindles into being and gives me a small flame of comfort. It looks like a tiny sprite – perhaps a Green Fairy, to guide me tonight. I pin it to my cravat with the beak to the left and look at myself in the dark mirror. I look like Poe's ghost, the patron saint of Gothic writers. Or maybe Dracula. Then I remember: vampires don't do carrion. They feed on the living, not the dead. Just like Ulysses Parslow.

I creep out of the dormitory like Nosferatu's shadow.

I know the way to the cemetery all too well. But it hits different going alone, and at night. Halfway there it occurs to me that this is a terrible pledge to begin my covert recording. I'm essentially going alone, and all there'll be for my pigeon skull to record will be me trespassing on the property of Yale Medical School. I make a mental note to record the Porphyria letter later. I have deliberately ignored The Gloomth instruction to destroy all their communications, and kept every one of them. I'll do a video when I get back to school.

*If* I get back to school.

I don't go to the grave I've visited many times, but the tomb I've only visited once. Somewhere on the way through the headstones I start to narrate – not necessarily as a conscious decision, but as a way to comfort myself as I pick my way through the dead. Because I'm interrogating every shadow, every hiding place behind trunk and tomb, I notice much more than I've ever done before.

'It's funny how people are as competitive with their houses when they are dead as when they are alive,' I whisper to myself.

'I mean, look at these tombs. Angels, Greek columns, even pyramids. It's like the houses in the Hamptons – whose is the biggest, whose is the fanciest. The old New England families still trying to outdo each other in death as they did in life.'

When I arrive at Theophilus Eaton's tomb, it's all I can do to shift the heavy stone from the top. Last time I did this there were seven of us – this time it's only me. In the end, I have to shove it sideways, just enough for me to squeeze through and drop down on to the stone staircase. As I descend once more into the underworld, it occurs to me that I should have brought my phone with me to use as a torch. But at New Haven, where rules surrounding tech are so strict, I've got out of the habit of carrying it. But I need not have worried. The brick-lined steam tunnels have low lights of sodium yellow enclosed in wire cages – or rather sulphur yellow, the colour of hellfire.

I walk through the wide atrium where we had the Squab dinner. There is no evidence now of our revelry except a stray champagne bottle, empty and on its side. Tonight there is no confusion of the kind I experienced in the chapel crypt – the right tunnel is clearly signposted with the Yale Med insignia of a serpent, rod and cross, and the words YALE UNIVERSITY SCHOOL OF MEDICINE. Evidently, donated bodies are taken straight from the cemetery's chapel of rest to the morgue, to be dissected by baby surgeons. I follow the signs for what seems like hours but can only have been about ten minutes, at every moment fearing and hearing the rumble of a trolley carrying a dead person, pushed by a live one. I soon come to a metal door with the same signage, same insignia. It is firmly locked, with a nine-digit keypad off to the side. Maths was never my strong suit but even

I know that nine numbers must have thousands of combinations, so I don't even try.

*Shit.*

Just as I'm rolling my eyes I see the metal frame of a vent above the door. A breeze comes from somewhere, and the low hum of an electric motor.

Aircon.

Somehow I find finger- and toeholds in the ancient brick and pull at the vent. It comes open along a hinge, and I scramble into it. Once again, I'm in a tunnel, a much tighter one this time. I don't do well with enclosed spaces. I see a cold bright light at the end of the tunnel, and crawl towards it, the irony not lost on me. There's another metal grid, and now I'm looking down into a sterile-looking white room. It could be a ward, as there are patients resting in beds.

But these aren't living patients, and those aren't beds.

They are the dead, laid out on slabs, and their rest is eternal.

I push the grille outwards, and I have no choice but to slide out head first like a diver, hands out to break my fall. I pick myself up and brush the worst of the brick dust from my uniform. I don't know what the Committee of Taste would make of me now.

The first thing I notice is the cold. It is absolutely frigid in here, like being in an icebox. My breath smokes and my fingers tingle. I bless the instinct that led me to put on my sweater. I only wish I'd brought gloves.

I don't know what I'd expected. Actually, I do – I thought everyone would be in those metal drawers that you pull out of the wall like you see on crime shows. I didn't expect them all to be on show like this, on their own little marble-top kitchen islands, an archipelago of the dead. Presumably it's so the students can gather around each subject. By the side of them all, a fibreglass skeleton hangs from a stand, mocking them all with his fleshlessness. 'You will all come to be like me in time,' his toothy grin seems to say. 'All shall resemble me.' As if to underline his point, a clock ticks relentlessly on the wall, counting down my mortality.

I walk along the rows. All human death is here.

I read names tied to big toes – I'm in the company of George, Leopold, Olivia, Herm, Manuel, Emily. And not all the cadavers came to a natural end, not all of them even enjoyed their three score years and ten or whatever you're supposed to be allotted in this life. There's a girl here, looks like teens or early twenties. MADISON GREEN, says the toe tag. She has a cloud of blonde hair, which spills over the cold, unforgiving marble like sunbeams. So might Porphyria have looked, when her lover strangled her with her own tresses. He went on to spend the night with her, but I avert my eyes from her body. I'm suddenly afraid for Harper again. Would Ulysses still love her like this? Would his obsession transcend the grave?

I turn away abruptly and walk the other way. Here are some more damaged souls – the students have been at work here and there are cavities where organs used to be, like a Victor Frankenstein has come along to harvest enough to make a human. The atrocities are casually covered by blue medical paper – with enough precision to keep the sites protected, not quite enough to prevent my eyes from seeing the horror.

Then the cruellest sight of all.

I look upon a face I know.

A face seen most recently in a sheaf of photographs Harper gave me. A dossier that went from girlhood to old-ladyhood, like someone else's life flashing before your eyes. A life that ended up here, on this slab. The shock of recognition hollows out my own insides, and a toe tag proclaims the worst:

BELINDA 'BUNNY' VAN BUREN

# 6

It feels deliberate.

It *must* be deliberate.

Bunny Van Buren.

My – Brat's – great-aunt.

They knew I had to come here, and they wanted her to be waiting for me.

And yet it doesn't make sense. If Ulysses Parslow knows, as he says he does, that I'm an imposter, why bother? Why present me with the ultimate Gothic horror of a much beloved, long-dead aunt to be my bedfellow?

I look closely at the familiar face. The cheeks have fallen in, the eye sockets are hollow. Papery wrinkles map the skin, and the grey hair is loose. In the photos it was always in a disciplined bun at the nape of her neck. I can't look at the rest of her body. She would never have wanted to be seen like this, without the Chanel and the family pearls.

I know, of course, that Bunny Van Buren had donated her body to medical science, and left a significant donation to Yale Med, one day, doubtless, to build the Belinda Van Buren Wing.

And the slab next to hers is empty – an opportunity for Brat to cuddle up with her one last time. For all I know this is part of the challenge, so I climb up there and lie straight, arms to the sides, just like she does. Correct and upstanding in death as she was in life, posture ramrod straight and perfect, like she was still a girl at Miss Cordelia's Academy in Hamden, walking the parlour with a pile of books on her head.

I lie straight in her honour, sudden, unbidden tears leaking from my eyes and running into my ears. I don't sleep. I'm not afraid any more, now that she's beside me. I'm not afraid of any of them, not the harmless dead. By tangling with The Gloomth, I'm riding into the valley of death's shadow, and this time I'm doing it willingly.

There's no way to see the sunrise in the windowless morgue. But when the clock shows seven, I figure that I am safe in terms of The Gloomth, but in increasing danger of some morgue attendant showing up to work.

As stiff and cold as the corpses around me, I rise from my slab. I shake myself off, doing some star jumps to coax my vessels back to life. Last night I went to some dark places – murky corners of my mind I never want to visit again. And it comes to me that I never want anyone else to experience that. With a flash of inspiration, I strip off the soccer sweater that probably saved me from hypothermia and dress the skeleton in it. Then I grab a pile of kidney dishes and arrange them into a winking smiley face on the floor. Someone will see them and know there has been a break-in – some prank or hazing ritual. They will tighten the morgue security, and Jess and Calvin will not have to experience the nightmare I just endured.

Furthermore, the boys will be eliminated from the pledging process, and saved from any further trials and whatever new devilry The Gloomth have dreamed up.

Before I scramble up into the vent, I hesitate, turn and kiss Bunny's cold forehead. It's just something I feel I have to do – to tell her goodbye.

As it turns out, my actions only save one of my fellow Squabs. A day or two later Calvin is brought back to school by a State Trooper. He'd been caught breaking into Yale Med – turns out they'd increased security following a student prank earlier in the week. He is given a principal's warning, and we are all treated to a lecture from Dr Gordon in Convocation about the seriousness of trespassing.

Jess, however, does succeed in spending the night in the morgue. The morning after his adventure I fall in to step with him on the way to the boathouse. He looks vampire pale, and not at all like he can work an oar today.

'How d'you pull it off?' I ask him as we walk through the fallen leaves to the boathouse.

'My older brother has a friend in Freshman Med,' he yawns. 'He got me a white coat and snuck me into an anatomy class, and I just hid after the lecture and stayed.'

Turns out Jess had a better experience than me – he'd hidden in the supply cupboard and spent the night eating candy and scrolling on his phone.

I'm still not entirely sure how The Gloomth know that Jess and I had spent the whole night there. The only way to be sure would be if there were security cameras. But I am pretty certain, having researched it, that cameras aren't allowed in Yale Morgue – something to do with laws surrounding human remains and it being a place of rest as well as a medical facility. Which means that, somehow, we are being watched.

I'd looked up the preservation of remains for medical research and didn't even have to go past the AI summary at the top to find out that bodies are kept for three years. So that *was* Bunny Van Buren – I hadn't had some chloroform-induced nightmare.

'Did you sleep?' I ask Jess.

'Not a wink,' he says. 'There was no way I was shutting my eyes in that place. That's why I went in the cupboard. I couldn't be in a room with . . . *them*. And even then, I felt like they were crowding outside the door, like some zombie movie.'

He laughs at himself, entirely unconvincingly. I see his face twitch, and the hand he pushes through his red hair shakes. I was wrong – he'd been changed by his experience too. I watch Calvin in the distance, on his own, kicking chestnuts savagely. He's been broken by rejection, and Jess will be broken by acceptance. Once again my heart hardens against The Gloomth. This cycle of abuse ends now.

# PART 6

## Hero and Leander

'Then dreadful thoughts of death, of waves heaped on him,
And friends, and parting daylight, rush upon him.'
*Hero and Leander* – Leigh Hunt, 1819

# 1

Now I'm anxious to get to the next pledge. I don't feel dread any more. I've mounted my steed and I'm ready to charge.

But of course, now I'm primed and ready for this to be over, there's a wait of about a week. I make recordings of the letters I've got from The Gloomth and recharge my tiny camera. I wonder what Anna made of the footage from the morgue. She would have seen my journey through the steam tunnels and then seen hours of white roof tiles while I laid down and she would have heard me talking to myself through the night.

God knows what I said – a dark stream of consciousness. Well, not so much a stream as a river – the River Styx between the living and the dead. I wish I could see her and talk again. That one conversation we had while dancing was so short, but so . . . valuable. I feel like I need a friend. But meeting up with anyone from *The Star* would be too risky at this stage. There is everything to lose.

Finally, finally, we have our next class with Lewis Walpole. And the title he chalks upon the board is all too familiar to me:

# HERO AND LEANDER

## By

### Leigh Hunt

Suddenly I'm in a dream, standing in Yale Art Gallery, looking at each brushstroke of a painting that was inspired by a poem which came from a legend. I'm looking at the black and boiling sea, the naiads holding Leander's head above the current, Hero waiting for her love on the shore.

'Mr Van Buren? I think you can explain this poem to us.'

It is a test. Ulysses turns right round in his chair and looks at me with his silver gaze. He wants to know how well briefed I am.

'It's the story of the ancient Greek legend of Leander, who swam a treacherous stretch of water called the Hellespont in order to meet with Hero, his lady love.' I try to remember Harper's words when we met in the gallery, and quote them faithfully. 'He drowned, and Hero threw herself into the water too. There's a picture, by Peter Paul Rubens, in Yale Art.'

'Yes,' says Lewis Walpole, looking at me closely. 'Yes, there is.' He walks to the corner of the classroom and opens a square mahogany cabinet that I've never seen before. Inside is an ancient gramophone with a wide brass trumpet. It's the most New Haven thing I've ever seen. The professor selects a vinyl disc and sets it on the turntable.

'While I tell you the legend,' he says, 'I would like to play you a rather special piece of music. There.' The record spins and an ethereal choral piece fills the room, bringing to mind wild waves and strange sea creatures. The professor begins to speak in a mannered, dramatic fashion, transporting us back through the centuries. From anyone else, it would sound ridiculous. From him, it's mesmeric.

'Across the Hellespont faced two cities – Abydos on one side and Sestos on the other. There lived a young woman called Hero in Sestos. Her golden hair shone as brightly as Apollo's brilliant sun, and her locks stole away the mind of anyone who gazed upon her, but she was a priestess in the service of Aphrodite, goddess of love, and had sworn in childhood never to marry. And in Abydos lived a young man called Leander. He walked tall, and as straight as a wand, and his shoulders were as broad as a warrior's. Well, fate drew them together at a feast in Sestos, and Leander fell in love at first sight. But when he tried his luck, Hero told him she could not return his affections as she had made an oath to Aphrodite. To which Leander said: "Do not tell me that you are bound by a promise that was made when you were too young to know better." It was agreed that if he could swim the Hellespont and meet her at midnight then they would steal away together and marry. Hero returned to Sestos with her priestesses, and that night Leander set off to swim the treacherous stretch of water.'

I look around the classroom. The Gothic Boys, as well as the rest of the class, are rapt – such is the spell the professor weaves that they are giving him their full attention.

'It so happened that Poseidon, the sea god, looked up from the swirling depths and caught sight of a swimmer in his domain. Poseidon conjured a storm from nowhere and used his trident to drag Leander down to his palace. There, the mighty sea god embraced him like a lover, finding the young man so beautiful he offered him immortality if he would stay in his watery kingdom for eternity. Leander confessed that he had sworn to the woman he loved that the waves of the sea would not keep him from her. Impressed by this fidelity, Poseidon agreed to release Leander, but warned him that without the protection of the gods he was risking his life. Sure enough, Leander drowned on the treacherous crossing, and Hero cast herself into the waves to join him in death.'

The faraway look fades from the professor's eyes, and the actor tone from his voice vanishes. Lewis Walpole is back in the room. He takes the needle from the record, the siren song ends and the spell is broken. 'And that,' he says, 'was the "Orphic Hymn to Poseidon". Quite the ditty, isn't it?'

He walks back to the chalkboard. 'In 1810 the great poet Lord Byron – bosom friend of Percy Bysshe Shelley – went to the Hellespont, now in modern Turkey, and swam the straits in one hour and ten minutes. He claimed that it was his greatest achievement, above any of his writings, because legend told that only the gods could swim the Hellespont.'

He taps the name on the blackboard, making a little snowstorm of chalk dots. 'It is said that this sporting feat inspired another poet in his circle – Leigh Hunt, to write this very poem in 1819. Now.' He collects the room with a glance, and points his famous chalk at all of us in turn. 'Byron swam the Hellespont for honour and glory. Both fine objectives. But I want you to ask yourselves: who, or what, would *you* cross the Hellespont for?'

Ulysses is the first to answer. 'Love,' he says simply.

'Just like Leander,' says Lewis Walpole. 'And you, Mr Van Buren?' I deliberately don't look at Ulysses. It's in my mind to say *hate* but I don't. I raise my hand to the comforting disc of the Van Buren medallion beneath my tie, visualise the two houses of its emblem.

'Rivalry,' I say. 'I would do it to beat someone else.'

'Interesting,' says Lewis Walpole, looking from one to the other of us. 'Would this epic battle be for the hand of . . . what did you call it . . . a lady love?'

'Oh, I think so,' I say lightly. I know Ulysses was talking about Harper, and I'm in the mood to goad him.

'All right, boys,' says the professor, dropping us as abruptly as a cat might drop a mouse he is torturing. 'Enough philosophising. Let's read.'

I wait my turn and read my verse, perhaps the most Gothic one of all:

> *Then dreadful thoughts of death, of waves heaped on him,*
> *And friends, and parting daylight, rush upon him*
> *He thinks of prayers to Neptune and his daughters,*
> *And Venus, Hero's queen, sprung from the waters;*
> *And then of Hero only,—how she fares,*
> *And what she'll feel, when the blank morn appears;*
> *And at that thought he stiffens once again*
> *His limbs, and pants, and strains, and climbs,—in vain.*
> *Fierce draughts he swallows of the wilful wave . . .*

Somewhere during that final line it dawns on me with absolute certainty what the next pledge will be. As I put my book down, I tune out the other boys' voices and my gaze drifts out of the window.

There, beyond the trees, is New Haven Lake.

The letter is there, waiting at bedtime, skewered to the pillow as before by a pigeon feather.

I take out the feather and read the writing.

*This is the second of three
Cardinal elimination challenges.*

*Meet at eleven o'clock on the
south shore of New Haven Lake.*

*You must reach the north shore by midnight.*

*It is time to swim the Hellespont.*

And, at the bottom, the direction: **<u>Full Gloomth Uniform Will Be Worn</u>**

Here is a difficulty. This letter, like the others, includes the dress code. I can't imagine we'll be swimming in the full uniform, but if we undress that means the pigeon skull camera won't be with me. And if I have to swim with it on, then the camera will be ruined by the water. It's a lose–lose and means another pledge that won't be properly recorded. This plan of Harper's is on fumes.

I suddenly have an idea: I find a pen and as insurance I scribble on the back of the letter: *IF ANYTHING HAPPENS TO ME CONTACT THOMPSON & FRENCH LAW FIRM.* I can't say it out loud because of the other boys in the dorm, but I hold it high in in front of the pigeon skull at my throat, keeping it still for ten seconds, so Anna can get a good look.

'Did you get one of these?'

I jump. It's Jess, fully suited and booted, waving his letter.

'Yes,' I say, turning the page I'm holding so he can just see their writing, not mine.

'What do you—'

'Not here,' I say. 'Come to the cloister.'

A figure sits up in bed to watch us go. Calvin looks at us gloomily, like a dog at a butcher's window. He is now on the outside looking in.

Jess and I tiptoe down to the cloister. It's a good place to talk, because you can always see someone approaching from way off. We sit on the low wall, just where we once sat with Calvin, feeling his absence like a missing tooth.

'Look, sport,' I begin. 'I want to ask you a favour. And it's not for me, it's for you.'

He looks from the paper in his hands to me. 'What is it?'

'I want you to drop out.'

He looks at me, his eyes startled wide. '*What?*'

Now the expression changes. He looks at me like I'm his enemy. 'Oh, I get you. You just want me to drop out so it's more of a given for you. If I'm gone, they'll have to let you in without trying as they'll be desperate for even one pledge. We are in the elimination zone.'

I don't say what I'm thinking, which is that I don't see Jess as physical. I worry about his strength to cross the Hellespont. I don't know if he can make it. If it had been the sporty Calvin, six foot something and all muscle, I wouldn't have had cause to worry about him undertaking the crossing. But Jess is weedy and skinny and bookish, and if there is sand to be kicked in someone's face he is far more likely to be the kickee than the kicker.

'I haven't come all this way, gone through all that shit with the Green Fairy and the heart to quit now.' I've got to admire his fortitude, really.

'These are evil people, Jess. They might end up killing you. *Believe* me.'

'Look, Brat,' he says. 'You're forgetting I'm from an old New England family too. I know all about the Van Burens and the Parslows. You hate each other. Always have. Jeez, my own cousin Martha couldn't invite her oldest school friend to her own wedding because she was a Parslow and Martha was marrying a Van Buren.'

'Westley Van Buren,' I say, remembering the family tree. 'I know.'

'What I'm saying is,' Jess goes on, 'you are always going to hate Ulysses. But that doesn't make him an evil guy. Look. I'm never gonna win a sports scholarship and my grades are good but not exceptional. I don't want to be a mediocre man living a mediocre life. I want to join The Gloomth, and that's what I'm damned well going to do. Nice try though. *Sport*.'

And with that he gets up and strides away along the cloister, in the direction of the lake.

I wait, cold stone under me, cold air about me, cold foreboding within me. The other Squabs and I had never been true friends – how can you be friends when you don't tell people the whole truth? – but I did feel the loss of Calvin and now Jess. I wish I could explain to Jess that I am trying to save his life.

I wait for the chapel clock to strike quarter to eleven, then I set off for the lake. I walk away from the school and over the meadows, my feet crisping on the already frosting grass, and through the chestnut grove where the autumn leaves whisper behind my back.

As I emerge, the water is, somehow, darker than the night. On the shore four black figures loom like the Fates: the Gothic Boys and Jess, all in immaculate Gloomth attire. It's a freezing night, clear and crisp, and a full white orb above the water casts a moonglade on the surface, making it almost resemble ice. I imagine another lake in another time and another place and wonder how Ulysses can bear to look on the water.

I'm already cold, even in my Gloomth outfit. If Jess and I are compelled to swim the lake naked, it could literally be the death of us. But if we have to swim in black suits and silk shirts and tailcoats, the water will soak our clothes and pull us under. Either way, I know I must somehow contrive to take off the pigeon skull and leave it on the shingle, if possible at some point of vantage so it can film what follows. But then it occurs to me that even if I got to the other shore alive, they may disqualify me from the pledge for being improperly dressed. It's just the kind of thing The Gloomth *would* do.

My quandary is solved by Iggy. 'The Squabs must disrobe entirely,' he says sternly, dark brows drawn together. 'We will bring the uniforms to the far shore.'

For the second time in as many weeks, I find myself undressing in front of the Gothic Boys. It's even more uncomfortable than it was in the crypt of the chapel, purely because of the temperature. I've had a lifetime of New England falls – you pay for the beautiful sunshine during the day with the clear, cold nights. This fall is no exception. My flesh shrinks and the goosebumps rise with each centimetre I expose to the elements. The humiliation of nakedness isn't even on my radar this time. This is survival.

To compound the cruelty, we are forced to fold our clothes neatly in the biting wind and place them in tidy piles on the shingle. Regretfully, I place the little silver pigeon cranium precisely on top. I turn the camera's eye to the water, but without much hope that it will be able to capture any of what follows.

And then – the worst: we inch over the shingle, with pebbles like ice cubes, and where the waves that lap the water sting like acid. I will never be able to adequately describe how freezing this water is. It is so cold I feel like I'm being burned – dipped inch by inch in molten lava fit to separate me from my skin. When the water reaches my ribs, I begin to gasp, totally involuntarily, like a summer dog. I simply can't help it. The Gothic Boys watch from the shore, with fond malice.

Jess, who is smaller and slighter than me with less muscle, is suffering just as much, if not more. But, unlike me, he has obviously concluded that the only way to keep the blood even vaguely pumping is to plunge in all at once and swim as fast as he can. He begins to thrash, splashily and haphazardly, across the lake.

Steeling myself, I follow. The clean and swift front crawl I've been practising since swimming lessons as a child is a muscle memory, but I'm just hoping that my icy limbs will work for long enough to get me across. I follow the path the moon has made, interrupting the moonbeams, wondering if Leander did the same. I'm not sure what the cold is doing to the chemistry of my brain, but somehow I feel even more trippy than I did on the night of the Green Fairy. Suddenly I *am* Leander in the Hellespont, and Hero stands on the far shore, holding her arms out to me, her miraculous hair and the moonbeams somehow one. She has Anna's face. Halfway across I can no longer feel my feet or hands, but I do feel like I will make it. The water is smooth, and there are no towering waves or treacherous currents like in Peter Paul Rubens' picture. Nothing between me and victory.

But then I see the boat.

The boat overtakes us, and I see Lowell and Iggy at the oars, and Oliver holding a lantern high. The rowers park their oars and I hear the pop of a cork before I see Ulysses pouring champagne in flute glasses for the four of them. They are treating this like a regatta. We swim up to them as they drink and when we draw level, we can hear them all singing a strange and beautiful song. The refrain sounds familiar, and I realise it is the 'Orphic Hymn to Poseidon', the same melody that Lewis Walpole played us in the classroom earlier. Then, as we swim closer, I see something so unbelievable that I think the cold is making me hallucinate.

The Gothic Boys have *tridents*.

We try to swim past, but they begin to jab their three-pronged forks into the water, trying to hinder us, push us under. Next moment my head is below the waves, aching with cold and rage.

Of course they cheated.

Of *course* they did.

Why would I think The Gloomth would play fair and let this be a straightforward swim across the lake, our only enemies cold and cramp? Why wouldn't they stack the deck, load the dice, mark the cards?

I try to dodge the prongs, but it's no use. I dive down to the depths, in a shaft of light from the boat lamp, and my reaching fingertips touch something and recoil. A floating figure. Not Poseidon, nor Jess, but a child. A child, that looks like Ulysses and yet not, a child in an orange coat the colour of fire and ice skates like twin knives. She floats nearer to me, her dark hair like weed wreathed about her little head, face a deathly grey, her eyes closed. As I recoil in a panic, her eyes open to reveal sockets, empty except for a shoal of tiny silver fish that swim out of her hollow skull. I open my mouth to scream, and water floods in. Lungs bursting, I claw for the moonlight above and break the surface, but the trident plunges for me like a harpoon. I duck under the boat, swimming beneath its shadow to the port side. The Gothic Boys are all facing the other way, spear fishing for Jess. Free at last, I strike for the shore. I *have* to make it by midnight.

But somehow my limbs won't move. I tread water, something holding me still like an anchor. Not cramp, but morality. I turn back and swim to the threshing figure.

'Stop!' I yell, tongue and lips numb with cold, my voice blunted and changed. 'He's drowning!'

Either they don't hear me or they won't. The Gothic Boys continue to sing, and stab, and swill champagne.

Remembering those swimming lessons, and my lifesaver's badge, I reach for Jess's cold and slimy form. Struggling for purchase, I turn on my back, pulling Jess's now inert body on mine. I kick out for shore, the double effort so arduous that I begin to feel I can't make it. An image swims before my delirious eyes, as I look up at the moon and the night and stars, a beautiful face crowned by beautiful hair. Suddenly I find the strength I need. She is my siren, my Hero, and she is the one who brings me to my safe haven. When my head hits shingle I stand, dragging Jess's dead weight to shore. I turn him on his front and batter his back, until water blurts out of his mouth and he starts to moan.

The boat grates on to the shingle a moment later. The Gothic Boys disembark, far too casually for my liking.

'Well done,' says Ulysses as he strolls over to us through the shallows, draining a champagne bottle.

'He's not out of the woods yet,' I gasp.

'I didn't mean that,' he says. 'You alone made it. You are the only remaining Squab. The only one worthy to try and join our ranks.'

Suddenly I'm white hot with fury. 'And who,' I say, 'gives a shit about that right now?'

He looks at me steadily. 'I do.'

Ulysses hands me a pile of clothes with a silver skull on top. I take the pigeon head first and know at once that something's wrong. The head is too light – no camera.

'No,' I say hurriedly. 'Those aren't mine.' I take instead the pile of clothes Lowell is holding for Jess and pick up the reassuringly heavy little skull from the top. The empty cranium I give back to Ulysses.

Together we turn Jess on his back and, with great difficulty, haul the clothes on over his dripping body. Only once he's dressed do I dress myself, and that's almost as hard because my fingers are numb. In the light of the moon Jess looks deathly pale. 'We need to get help,' I say through chattering teeth. 'Does anyone have their phone? We need to call 911. We have to get him to Yale Med.'

'No,' says Ulysses. 'We'll take him to the infirmary.' He looks around at his acolytes. I suppose it's to their credit that the other Gothic Boys look a little unsure. The infirmary is the school's medical ward. It's fine for a bout of flu or a sprained ankle, but it's hardly Johns Hopkins.

'Are you kidding?' I sputter through chattering teeth. 'He needs an ambulance!'

'No EMTs,' Ulysses reiterates. 'They'll file a report, and then we'll all be in the shit. You can kiss the Ivy League goodbye.'

This convinces the others. All those boys are living for their college applications, their extra credit and the next rung on the ladder of their perfect lives.

'He's right,' says Iggy. 'No EMTs.'

'You're crazy,' I say. 'He needs medical help.'

'And he's going to get it from Matron. You need us to carry him back,' says Ulysses simply. 'So it's either our way, or he stays here.'

It's the difference between life and death. Jess would die of exposure by morning. I nod once, curtly, a pact of silence. Ulysses opens his hand to show us all the little silver pigeon head in his palm. Then I realise how lucky it was that I swapped the skulls around, because he turns and whips the thing out to the middle of the lake, where it lands in the silver path of the moon.

And I realise that what brought me to shore across those last terrible yards was not the image of Harper with her hair like moonbeams, but of Anna Sato, her hair like night.

We carry a dripping Jess between us – he stumbles, and we half drag him through the chestnut grove. *Not out of the woods yet*, I keep thinking, the old phrase suddenly literal. He is icy cold and delirious, mumbling about something and nothing and everything. The lights of the school lead us like the Bethlehem Star, and the warmth of the infirmary hits like hellfire. We deliver Jess to Matron, a comforting, motherly Black woman who reminds me of Stacey from Marty's Café.

'Too much champagne,' Ulysses tells her smoothly, 'and a swim he didn't plan to have. But if anyone can warm him up, you can.'

His charm kindles its own warmth, so much so that Matron actually smiles at him as she wags an admonishing finger.

'Ulysses Parslow, you are a mighty bad influence. Don't think I don't know about your boys and your pledges. Y'all get to your beds now. Leave him to me.' She folds Jess to her bosom, and I feel a small stab of envy, because I too would like to bury my cheek in her shoulder and sob. She beckons two orderlies over his head, and the three of them carry him off to bed.

As we walk out into the night, Ulysses throws an arm across my shoulder. 'Come for a nightcap. You've earned it.'

Incapable of forming the words to refuse, I allow myself to be led like a leaf in the current. I've always wondered where The Gloomth live, since they are not in the general dorm with the rest of us. The only evidence the Gothic Boys had ever even been in our dorm were the letters that appeared on our pillows. I assumed they'd have their own house, and evidently they did. But this was no comfortably dilapidated frat house such as you'd see on college campuses all across America, scarred and stained by too many keg parties. This was an elegant Jacobean lodge down beyond the boathouse, which looked like it might have been built when the first Jamestown settlers washed up in this country.

'Come to my rooms,' Ulysses says, letting us into the front door. 'You need a brandy.' The others make as if to follow, but are prevented by the lift of a white hand. 'No,' he says, 'just Brat.' The other Gothic Boys, who know not to argue, slope off to bed. The door closes behind them and Ulysses and I look at each other. We are alone, in his domain, like Leander and Poseidon.

The moment breaks. He goes to a mahogany closet and starts throwing clothes over his shoulder, the garments flying like birds. I attempt to catch them, with varying degrees of success. 'Put these on,' he says. 'I'll light a fire.' For a moment I think he's going to watch me undress again but he directs me to a bathroom, which has a marble bath with a dark wood surround and sporting prints on the wall.

I peel off my cold, damp Gloomth uniform and put on what he's given me. It feels strange sliding on a pair of Ulysses

Parslow's clean underpants. But I'm grateful for the thick button-down hunting shirt and corduroy trousers. There are warm socks too, and I have to make do with my own shoes, but they are all but dry by now. I take a look at myself in the mirror. Brat looks back. There's no trace, except the damp hair swept back from the forehead, and a wary look in the amber Van Buren eyes, of what he has been through tonight.

Mindful of the sartorial rules of looking after your Gloomth uniform I fold the dark clothes carefully and poise the silver pigeon skull on top, just as we had to leave them on the shingle. I check the camera – the tiny green light still shines. It's on.

As I emerge, Ulysses takes the pile from me. He's already in silk pyjamas and an embroidered dressing gown, looking like a beautiful vampire on his night off. 'I'll have them cleaned,' he says, 'now that you'll need them again.'

I watch the pigeon skull being carried away from me and my hand shoots out in a panic. 'I'll take this though,' I say. 'For safekeeping.'

'Yes,' he says. 'Best put it in your pocket.'

Under his eye, I've no choice but to slip the silver skull into the breast pocket of the flannel shirt. Now the pigeon eye can't see – but hopefully it can hear.

In the time it has taken me to change, Ulysses has built a merry fire that is burning in the grate and arranged a pile of silken cushions on the hearthrug. It looks like a date.

'Get yourself warm,' he says with an elegant, inviting sweep of his pale hand. I sit on the cushions, upright and uptight, feeling super awkward. In contrast Ulysses, with his natural grace, throws himself down on the cushions, like a reclining, dining Roman. He laughs at me. 'Relax,' he says. 'I won't bite.' It's as if he has read my mind, and the vampiric thought has somehow fluttered from my brain to his. Like a bat. I lean back on my elbow and look around me, taking in the incredible decor. The Committee of Taste has done its work. There is a marble bust, an ancient engraving of the city of Otranto, a stuffed pigeon in a glass case, and everywhere the most elegant furniture with carved spindles or inlaid wood. The room is crowded with things, a cabinet of curiosities. But it doesn't make the mistake of tipping over the top into vulgarity. There's no tackiness, just solid, classy quality. Ulysses reaches up to a side table to grab a bottle of brandy and two glasses the size of babies' heads. He pours me two fingers of tawny liquid.

'Here,' he says. 'For the shock.'

I drink the brandy straight down and he refills the glass immediately. By the time I'm outside of my second glass I stop shaking and start to feel something I never thought I'd feel again – warmth. I turn to my enemy, my fireside companion.

'Why are you being so nice to me?'

He doesn't answer directly but looks into the hearth, the firelight igniting the flaming beauty of his face. 'During the third crusade, King Richard the Lionheart became very ill with a fever after the Siege of Acre. His sworn enemy Saladin, instead of pressing his advantage and taking back the city, ordered a pause in hostilities and sent Richard melted snow from the slopes of Mount Simeon, and grapes from the vineyards of Damascus, to ease his fever. The point is, we can show courtesy even to our enemies.'

His voice is hypnotic. The combination of it, and the fire and the brandy, are almost sending me to sleep. 'I like your honesty,' I mumble.

'I like *you*,' he says. His hand travels over the fabric of the shirt, and for a dreadful moment I think he has somehow detected the camera in my pocket. But then his fingers slide between the buttons and caress my bare skin.

Suddenly I'm wide awake.

'When you were by the lake,' he murmurs, 'you looked like a statue. Leander in marble, by some attic sculptor.'

He's uncomfortably close, like he's whispering in my mouth. I realise his intention a second too late. The kiss is hotter than the fire.

I pull away, shocked and tingling. My first thought is that no one would believe this. There's no way the camera can have seen this from my pocket, so I have to find a way to articulate what happened for the reporters of the Ida Barney *Star*.

I say, 'How can you kiss a Van Buren?'

'But you are not a Van Buren, are you? I don't know who you are, but you are beautiful.'

I draw away from him, sit up.

He sighs and pours us another glass. 'It's such a shame you're not Brat,' he says lightly, conversationally. 'You are more worthy of the name Van Buren than he. Braver, more stalwart. *Much* more attractive.'

Suddenly I see an opportunity to drive a wedge between him and Harper, to stamp out the spark I thought I saw at the Feathers Ball. 'What about Harper? How would she feel about you kissing me?'

'I love Harper,' he says seriously. 'With a depth you'll never know. But even the greatest of lovers took lovers of their own. Percy Shelley and Mary Shelley were devoted, as you know – she held his heart in her hands in more ways than one. But they both slept with others in their circle – both men and women. Like the Romans, like the Greeks – they were never so bourgeois as to think that sex should be confined to one gender. You're not from our world so you don't understand. The rules don't apply to people like us.'

He takes another slug of brandy. 'Harper won't mind sharing. But I warn you – if the real Brat couldn't take her away from me, she certainly won't leave me for you.'

'Leave you? What are you talking about? Are you ... *with* Harper?'

'Always have been. Didn't you know? We are engaged.'

I'm reeling. 'You *can't* be engaged. You're eighteen.'

'You can get married at eighteen in the state of Connecticut,' he says. 'Besides, it's not a formal arrangement. It's an agreement between our families ever since we were small. You could say it's a literal interpretation of the word *intended*.'

Suddenly the words Lewis Walpole used to tell the story of Hero and Leander come back to me with stunning clarity. *'Do not tell me that you are bound by a promise that was made when you were too young to know better,'* I quote.

'That's exactly what I'm telling you.' He regards me with amusement, drinking in my discomfiture as he once drank my tears. Suddenly I can't be under his silver gaze any more. I set down my brandy glass on the hearth – the firelight turns the cut glass to a million yellow diamonds. So many riches in this room, too much, enough to turn the stomach.

I get up. 'Sorry. I have to get to bed.'

He gets up too, reluctantly, and follows me to the door. 'To be continued.'

On the threshold of night I turn to face him.

'Thanks for the clothes. I'll bring them back.'

But I don't thank him for the kiss, nor promise to return it.

As I walk back to the dorm I'm still trembling, whether from the kiss or the swim I don't know. I'm utterly spent and longing for bed, but at the same time my flesh is fizzing and burning, and my mind is churning with the incredible piece of information I just learned. Harper and Ulysses? Together all along? Not just an adolescent kiss on the ice but a betrothal, forged in childhood and binding into the future. Why didn't she tell me? I thought we were becoming friends.

I want to go to Ida Barney right now, run to her dormitory instead of mine and demand answers. But to do that would be to give everything away. I turn my footsteps to the main school. But just as when I crossed the lake and struck for home, I find myself changing direction involuntarily and head instead to the infirmary.

It's now the small hours, so there is no one on duty but the night nurses and porters. I slip past them and find the room where they put Jess. He's sleeping, his red hair rumpled on the pillow. I breathe relief and sit in the chair by his bedside, trying to gather my thoughts.

The first thought in the bunch is how much I would rather be here, in this sterile, disinfectant-smelling ward, than in that drawing room. At least here there is honesty, not the seduction of beautiful things. Jess's hand, still red and raw from the cold lake, lies outside the bedclothes. Gently, I take it. He must have felt the pressure, because his eyes flicker open. He registers me and speaks with the caw of a crow.

'You were right,' he croaks. 'They were trying to kill us.'

I lean forward, still holding his hand. 'Would you say something?' I whisper urgently. 'If I told someone, would you testify?'

He gives me a watery smile. 'No. If I did, they wouldn't let me try next year.'

It's no good. He's lost. I wait until he falls asleep. Then, as soon as I can, I drop his hand.

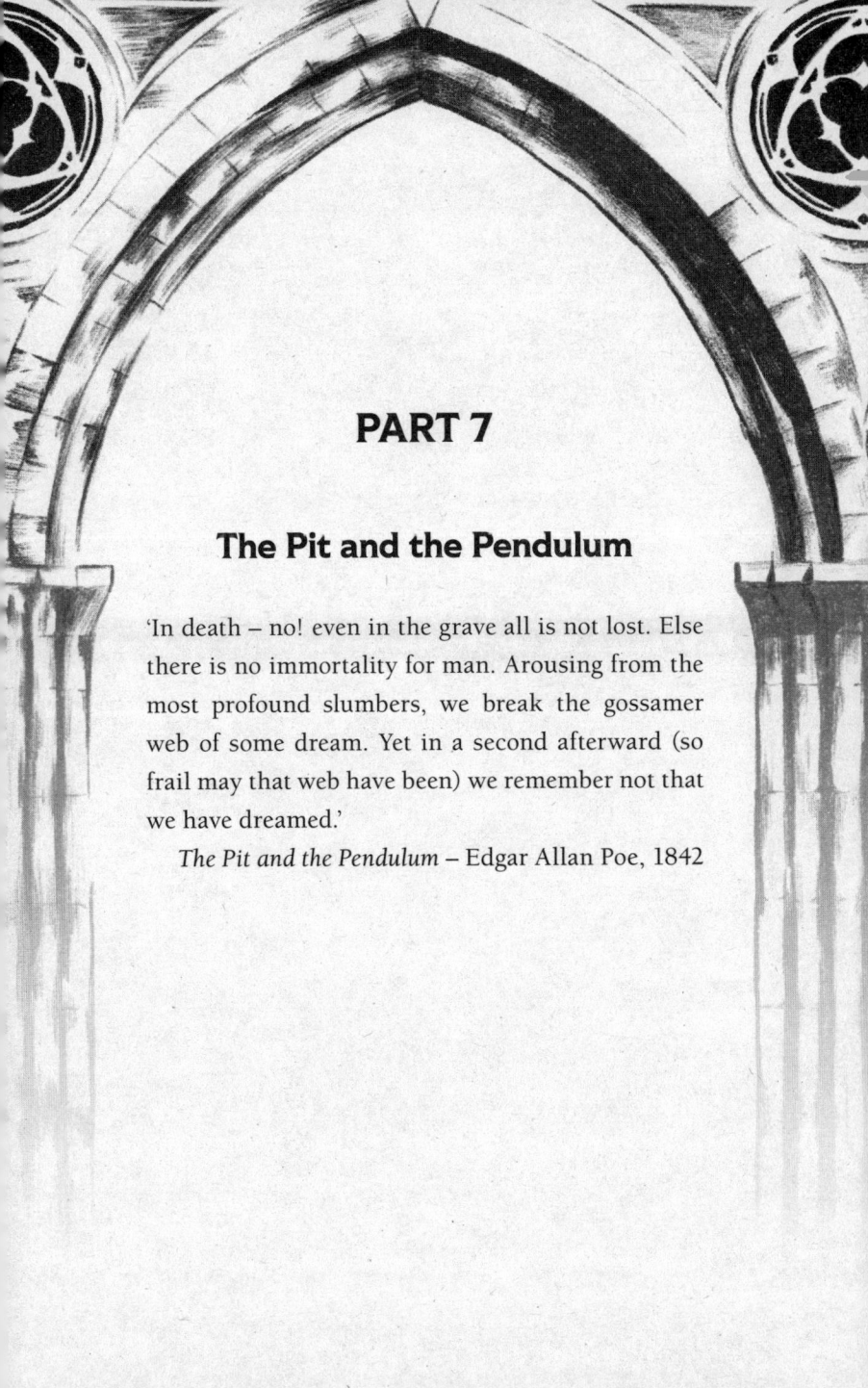

# PART 7

## The Pit and the Pendulum

'In death – no! even in the grave all is not lost. Else there is no immortality for man. Arousing from the most profound slumbers, we break the gossamer web of some dream. Yet in a second afterward (so frail may that web have been) we remember not that we have dreamed.'

*The Pit and the Pendulum* – Edgar Allan Poe, 1842

# 1

The next morning, I'm shattered. Not only was I up drinking brandy at 1 a.m., but my whole body aches from the sub-zero swim over the Hellespont. When I haul myself out of bed at the rising bell and stumble to the bathroom, the pigeon skull watches me. Even in my exhausted state, I'd remembered to put the camera on charge last night.

I look back at him, considering. I have a crucial message to send. But I can't exactly speak into the camera here, with all my dorm-mates listening, and even if I go to the john, they'll hear me talking to myself.

Then I remember.

*The phone.*

I get the phone Reuter gave me out of my nightstand drawer. Thank God, it still has juice. I look for a moment at the photo of Brat Van Buren on the home screen, then tap the Message app. There's only one contact in there, a simple star emoji to represent the team from Ida Barney.

**Harper**

I type.

```
meet me at Yale Art this evening
in front of Hero and Leander
5pm
don't fail me
the plan depends on it
```

My first class, of course, is literature with Lewis Walpole. And now, as we are getting to the final challenge of the pledge, I walk to class with the heavy heart of a prisoner about to be sentenced. As I am the one remaining Squab, the lesson, taught to twenty boys, will essentially be just for me. In it I will learn my fate – the last trial I need to endure before finally becoming a member of The Gloomth. It only now occurs to me too that this year The Gloomth have broken with tradition – for the first time they are not replacing their number. Usually there would be enough Squabs to take over when The Gloomth from the year above leave the school. This year they've made it difficult enough so there is only me left pledging. Why?

Unfortunately, I think I know.

As I walk from the dorm across the green lawns, a single pigeon accompanies me. We walk along quite companionably, and now I've lost my fellow Squabs I'm glad of him. His head jerks in and out as he walks, and the sun picks out the unexpected rose sheen on his pewter grey breast. Outside the refectory he joins a small group of other pigeons, pecking at a scatter of crumbs. I leave him to it and go into breakfast.

In class I take my place at the front, next to Ulysses Parslow. I'm the last to arrive, almost like the guest of honour, and I might be imagining it but it feels like everyone is looking at me expectantly. I glance at Ulysses. He gives me a sideways smile and a nod, but there is nothing in his expression that betrays what happened between us last night. I'm beginning to wonder if I imagined it all.

I am not kept in suspense for too long. As soon as Professor Walpole enters the room, he strides straight to the blackboard and chalks the three words that will dictate my fate, almost before he utters a 'good morning'.

## *EDGAR ALLAN POE*

I might have known, really. Poe is the Top Dog, the Bog Kahuna Burger, the Grand Fromage on Campus. 'It is now time to speak,' the professor says with reverence, 'of the great Edgar Allan Poe. The high priest of Gothic, the successor to my ancestor Horace Walpole and the very epitome of a Gothic writer. This, boys, is what we are here for – *this* is the man.' He looks excited, and somehow younger, as if the years have fallen away. His eyes shine, his pink tongue flicks out between the white beard like a lizard's as he speaks. Next moment he'll be licking his lips.

'You may be familiar with his short stories: *The Masque of the Red Death*, *The Fall of the House of Usher*, *The Tell-Tale Heart*.'

I know them all. *The Tell-Tale Heart*, of course, I remember very well. The tale of a murdered man buried beneath the floorboards, his still-beating heart giving his murderer away. That story unlocked the very first pledge for me, below the floorboards of the chapel.

'But today we are going to look at arguably the most famous, and arguably the most Gothic, of his stories – *The Pit and the Pendulum*. And today we are going to do something a little different. Stand behind your chairs, boys.'

We all get to our feet, and there is a scrape of chairs as we tuck them below our desks. 'Bring your Poes,' says Lewis Walpole, 'and come with me.'

We duly pick up our books and follow his striding figure out of the classroom and down the cloister, his black gown unfurling behind him like a raven's wing. Lewis Walpole moves at quite a lick for an elderly gentleman, and at times we would have lost him but for the black tail of his gown snapping round a corner. We trot to keep up, jostling after him into the wide stone doorway of the chapel. He marches unerringly to the hidden door and we clatter down the stone spiral staircase to the crypt.

'Form a circle, boys,' he commands, and we sit obediently, cross-legged, on the stone floor. He takes out a box of matches and strikes a light to the wicks of seven tall candles set about the place, so there is enough light to read.

'Mr . . . Parslow. A summary, please, of the plot of *The Pit and the Pendulum*. And please begin by answering the question: why have I lit seven candles?'

Of course it would be Ulysses.

'An unnamed prisoner is brought before the Spanish Inquisition, charged with crimes the nature of which we are never told,' he begins. 'You've lit seven candles because the duration of his trial is set as the time it takes for them to burn down. The narrator is condemned to death and he passes out from the shock, awakening to find himself in a totally dark room. At first the prisoner thinks that he is locked in his own tomb, but then he discovers that he is in a cell.'

I swallow, the panic rising in my chest. An underground tomb. I can't bear to even think of it.

'He decides to explore the cell and works out that the perimeter measures one hundred steps. By chance he trips and falls while crossing the room, and lands at the edge of what seems to be a vertiginous drop. He recognises with horror that if he hadn't fallen, he would have walked straight into a deep pit. He faints from terror at how close he came to death. When he wakes up he is strapped to a wooden frame, facing the ceiling. He can see a portrait of Father Time, and from it hangs a razor-sharp giant pendulum. The pendulum is slowly descending, slicing back and forth, designed to kill the prisoner. However, he is able to smear his bonds with the meat that has been left for him to eat. Rats are drawn to the smell, and as they gnaw the meat, they nibble through his straps too, setting him free seconds before the pendulum's blade slices him.'

Everyone in the crypt is listening, just like the morning when the professor told us about Hero and Leander, but today they are even more entranced, possibly because of our Gothic location.

'Free from his bonds, the prisoner thinks he is safe. But he soon realises that the walls of his dungeon are becoming fiery hot, and moving inwards, causing the cell to shrink. He is forced to the middle of the room and there is nowhere to go but the pit. Just as he begins to fall in, an arm pulls him to safety.

The French Army has captured the city and the Inquisition has fallen.'

'Good,' says Lewis Walpole. 'Now let us read. And this time, because we too are in a subterranean space, I want you to *feel* the darkness and the terror. If you wish to weep, then weep.' Again, his enthusiasm is uncalled for. 'Mr Arblaster, start us off.'

Oliver begins to read, and I listen with a growing sense of horror. It is a truly terrifying tale. I have been on a solid diet of Gothic since I enrolled at the university of Harper Larsson, but somehow this short story hits me harder than anything else I've read. Maybe it's our location, maybe it's the writing, but I feel, as the voices of my classmates echo around the crypt, whispering round and back to us like a multitude, that I almost can't bear it any more. Jess, two spaces along from me, starts to snivel, and Lewis Walpole pounces on him like a raptor.

'Good,' he says, caressing Jess's freckled cheek and touching his tears. 'Good. You are feeling Gloomth right now.'

I'm pretty sure that Jess's misery is all wrapped up in the disappointment that he failed the pledge, rather than in the dark rapture of Poe's work, but I don't think the reasons would alter the professor's delight. At his oh-so-evident approval, I hear more sniffs and sobs from around the room, as other boys give way to tears. It's like some horrible contagion, a collective hysteria like the fake witches of Salem. And it's over this tide of Gloomth that I must make myself heard – as usual, I am given the horrible climax of the story to read, and as I embark on my chapter I almost can't trust my voice. It sounds weedy and wavering and scared. It falls to me to read what the prisoner believes to be his final moments, when the fiery walls close in to force him down into the pit to his death.

'*I could have clasped the red walls to my bosom as a garment of eternal peace. "Death," I said, "any death but that of the pit!" Fool! might I have not known that into the pit it was the object of the burning iron to urge me?*'

'Exquisite,' says Lewis Walpole, feeding off the fear in my voice. 'And I think the final stanza, when the trumpets of France signal the fall of Toledo, should rightly be read by Señor Ignatio Jorquera.'

Iggy draws his dark brows together, straining to read as the last candle burns down.

'*No es que me atemorizara mirar cosas horribles, sino que me aterraba la idea de no ver nada.*'

'Which translates as?'

Iggy thinks for a moment. 'It's not that I was afraid of looking at horrible things, but I was terrified of the idea of not seeing anything.'

The professor nods sagely. 'What is the poet speaking of?'

The last candle dies, with a smoky smell of Christmas and church and the going away of everything light and good in the world.

We sit in the dark, saying nothing. Lewis Walpole whispers the answer, which reaches us on the wings of an echo.

'He speaks of the ultimate blindness of death.'

Afterwards, we have the shock of finding out that it is still daylight, like when you leave a movie theatre after watching a horror film at noon. The rest of the day drags on, and it seems an eternity until my meeting with Harper. But at last school's out, and I swerve study hall and go to the dorm instead to change out of my uniform. And there, on the bed, speared to the pillow with a pigeon feather, is the final letter.

*THE GLOOMTH SOCIETY*

*Cordially invites you to:*

*THE ANNUAL GLOOMTH DINNER*

*On Saturday 24th October 2026*

*At Strawberry Hill Villa*

*New Haven, Connecticut*

> *The third and final Cardinal challenge will take place during the courſe of the evening*
>
> *Carriageſ depart New Haven ſchool at 5 p.m.*
>
> <u>*Full Gloomth Uniform Will Be Worn*</u>

Tomorrow. The final pledge is tomorrow. I swallow. I had not thought it would be so soon.

Only a daredevil would enter that place knowing what I know, and having read what I read this morning in class. But I have nothing visual on camera and can prove nothing about the night of the Hellespont. I *have* to go. I *have* to finish this. I think of Jess's tears this morning and how he wouldn't be crying if he knew what he had escaped.

It is a trap, a trap sprung just for me, and I have to walk into it willingly.

I stuff the letter into my pocket and clatter down the back stairs. As I hurry down the school drive, at every moment expecting a voice to call me back, I notice that the pecking pigeons from this morning have swelled in number – there are about a hundred congregating on the chippings. I scatter them with my feet as I go, and they rise and return like memories.

# 3

I get into Yale Art Gallery on the last admission of the day.

As before, I find my way unerringly to *Hero and Leander*. Harper is there, all blonde beauty, standing in front of the Rubens. But she's somehow cold, like the moon in the painting, not warm like the sun. She greets me coldly too, not saying anything, and wears an unreadable expression. But there's no time to decode her mood. We are entering the season finale of The Gloomth pledges. For a brief moment I ponder whether to task her first with what I know about her and Ulysses, but then I unfold the letter and wave it under her nose.

'It's showtime, Scoop,' I say. 'I've been invited to Strawberry Hill Villa. Tomorrow. That's Lewis Walpole's house, right? Look.' I jab the paper with my forefinger. 'It says the final Cardinal challenge will take place during the course of the evening. We're in the endgame.'

Still she says nothing.

'And,' I say, 'they've eliminated *all* the others this year. They aren't replacing their number. Which means they are planning something just for me.'

'I'm not sure what that has to do with me, *Eddie Dontay*.'

I'm thrown by the use of my alias after such a long time, spoken with such volume and emphasis. I look around. 'Shh. Someone will—'

She doesn't let me finish. 'Or should I say Edmond Dantès?'

I go still.

'Or more accurately: Bartholomew Van Buren III?'

I straighten, and sigh. It's over. 'Who told you?'

'Your lawyer.'

'My *lawyer*?' I repeat. I don't want to say too much. I want to see how much she knows.

'Or rather, *both* your lawyers.'

Harper gets a paper from her pocket. 'This contract you signed. You say that the state's lawyer would vouch for you. Stevie did your ID check with the firm you gave us, Thompson & French. They vouched for you verbally over the phone, so we went ahead with the sting. But they also said they would send a written testimonial through the mail – obviously they are old school – and that's only just arrived. Here's the reference we got, signed by the senior partner, Noah Thompson. He said you were who you said you were; everything was hunky-dory.'

I hold my tongue.

'Only trouble is, Stevie noticed something. She recalled that when she wrote to the school on the headed notepaper of the Van Buren family lawyer, one Theodore Seamark, she duplicated the laser pen signature.' Harper unfolds another paper and holds the two pages side by side. 'And gosh darn it, you'll never guess what we found.'

I could guess. I could guess very well. But I obligingly lean in and read both signatures.

## *Theodore Seamark*   *Noah Thompson*

'You see the S that's written like an F? That's Gloomth handwriting.'

I can't deny it.

'Mr Seamark was obviously a member of The Gloomth. Not so surprising, considering that your late great-uncle Jebediah Van Buren, his bosom friend and boss, was a Gloomth member too, and left his fortune to the society if he died without heirs. But would Noah Thompson, a pro bono state lawyer from a two-bit law firm be a member of The Gloomth too? We thought that was too much of a coincidence. So Stevie ran an AI graphology programme, to analyse the signatures. And whaddya know?' She scrumples up the two pages together. 'Same. Exact. Guy.'

Still I say nothing, but my mind is racing, a lab rat in a maze, trying to find a way out of this one.

'Then,' she goes on, 'I looked at the contract you signed. She shows me a third page. 'You remember filling this in for me?'

It's not a question that requires an answer.

She reads the contract out:

'Name: Edmond Dontay. Address: 34 Wilmore. Character referee: Abbot Faria – according to you a priest at the mission. ID check: Thompson & French, Attorneys-at-Law – who you said were the pro bono lawyers of the family court. So I googled the names. And what did I find?'

This is clearly a rhetorical question. 'Edmond Dantès is the main character in *The Count of Monte Cristo*. An innocent sailor from Napoleonic France framed for a crime he didn't commit. He spends fourteen years on the notorious Château d'If island fortress, known simply as Prisoner 34. There he befriends a fellow prisoner, an abbot called Faria. The abbot tells him about a treasure island called Monte Cristo, and once Dantès escapes he goes to the island to claim the fabulous wealth and recreate himself. Now rich enough to exact revenge on those who wronged him, he takes the alias Wilmore, and engages lawyers called Thompson and French.' She takes a beat. 'You'd constructed a whole fictitious world for yourself from Brat Van Buren's favourite book.'

'Harper—'

She cuts me off. 'You came looking for me, didn't you? With your tan and your bleached surfer hair and your hard-luck story. You knew I was the editor of *The Star*, because I told you last fall, on our date. You needed me to investigate your story.'

She throws the ball of paper at my head. I put up my hand and catch it before impact. I hold her gaze with mine, defiant, my fist next to my temple.

'My murder,' I say quietly. 'I needed you to investigate my *murder*.'

'What are you talking about?'

'You said The Gloomth had done something to scare Brat. You were right. They killed him. Ulysses killed him. *Me*.'

'*No*.' She backs away. 'Ulysses wouldn't do that. The others I believe. But not him. You're caught up in this ridiculous Van Buren/Parslow feud.'

'Are you in love with him?' The question comes out before I've had a chance to edit it.

'No, of *course* not,' she says. 'He's just an old friend.'

'You're not engaged then? Because *he* seems to think you are.'

She has the grace to blush. 'That old nonsense. It's just a family joke.'

'Well, he seems to take it pretty seriously.' Now she's silent. I take a step towards her, towards the painting. 'Let me tell you what I think happened. You've known Ulysses since forever, and you've been bound together since that tragic first kiss. But then he joined a secret society he wouldn't tell you about and maybe you got the feeling he was sleeping around. You got caught up with Brat, felt drawn to him, thought he might be your way to get over Ulysses. Brat took you to the Feathers Ball, and you told him that you disliked Ulysses, that he was a dick. But then Brat let you down too, or rather, stood you up. Once he'd left town, you began to pine for Ulysses. And when a Brat Van Buren lookalike turned up, you were at last going to find out about The Gloomth and make your name on the newspaper. Then at the Feathers Ball you saw Ulysses again and fell harder than ever. So did he. Does this sound at all possible to you?'

'Don't try to deflect,' she says. 'I'm done with you. *We're* done with you. We're all disgusted with you – me, Reuter, Stevie and Anna.' This last one stings. 'You *used* us. Why would you *do* that?'

Stacey from the café's phrase comes back to me. *You gotta do what them pigeons do. Shit on everyone else before they shit on you.* I didn't want to shit on Harper, or the team. But I had to do it, to get what I wanted. And now they hate me. I don't so much mind Harper thinking me a Judas, but I very much mind Anna thinking it.

'I'll answer that one if you answer me another. If you'd known I was going after Ulysses Parslow, would you have helped me?'

She doesn't reply, doesn't look at me. She looks frightened. And I get it. She thought she was getting into a lurid story about hazing, and suddenly she's got a murder exposé on her hands.

I try one last desperate time. 'Look, Harper. The Gloomth buried me alive last year. And if they try to kill me again this year, I *am* going to expose them, with or without you. Will you help me?'

She hesitates. Then she shakes her bright head. 'I'm sorry. I trusted Eddie Dontay, but I just can't trust Brat Van Buren, The Count of Connecticut. And I'll have our camera back, please.' She held out her hand.

I think fast. 'It's already wrecked,' I say. 'I wore it for the Hellespont challenge and it went in the lake. It hasn't worked since.'

She shrugs. 'Then you really are on your own.'

Seamark's law firm is closing up for the evening. The receptionist, Mae, is putting on her lipstick and fluffing out her hair, but I don't care. Full of righteous fury, I march right past her without announcing myself. She knows who I am anyway. She's known me ever since I was a kid, and I used to come here with my Great-Uncle Jebediah and play on her revolving chair.

I burst into Theodore Seamark's office, slamming the door behind me so hard that his framed law school certificates nearly jump off the wall.

'You couldn't change your signature?!'

Seamark is pretty unshockable. He screws the cap on his fountain pen calmly before greeting me.

'Hello, Brat.'

I don't greet him back. 'A *year* of planning, and living as Eddie Dontay, and working at Marty's Café, and you couldn't change your goddamned *signature*?'

'What are you talking about?'

I unfurl the paper from my pocket and smooth the two photocopies out on to his mahogany desk. He peers at them.

Then he sets the pen down on the leather topper of his, with the air of a murderer laying down a smoking gun. 'Oh.'

'Yes,' I say. 'Oh.'

I fling myself into the chair across from him. I don't mention that it was my own foolishness, my own whim to use characters and aliases from *The Count of Monte Cristo* that had confirmed my true identity. Right now, I just need someone else to blame.

'And now,' I say, 'Harper's cut me loose. Which places me in considerable danger. They gave me a tiny camera, and a GPS tracker, but now I'm on my own.'

Seamark strokes his clean-shaven chin. 'You still have the camera?' he asks.

'I *physically* have it, yes. But that's no use if there's no one on the other end.' I think of Anna, our brief, electric connection. Then I think of her just turning off my feed, leaving me to burn.

'And you have the GPS?'

I flick the Van Buren medallion out of the neck of my hoodie. 'It's here. But who's going to track it? You?'

He sits back in his chair, deep in thought.

'Couldn't we go to the police now?' I suggest. 'Tell them what I'm going to do. Have *them* track me?'

He shakes his grey head. 'As I told you a year ago, there is no way the police department would agree to this. It's what we in the legal profession call entrapment. Plus, they would never mount a sting operation in the property of one of the foremost philanthropists of New Haven society, Lewis Walpole. And not forgetting your own status. They would never let the Van Buren heir place himself in danger.'

'Which is why I got the Ida Barney *Star* team involved in the first place. That's why you got me the job at the Commencement

Dinner. They were happy to help the broke loser Eddie Dontay. But now they've found out I'm Bartholomew Van Buren III they've dropped me like a hot coal.'

He chews his lip.

I lean forward. 'Seamark,' I say. 'You said yourself we can't take The Gloomth on without evidence. I *have* to go and see if they will try to kill me again.'

He is silent.

'You tell me. You tell me if there is another way.'

Seamark sighs. 'Your great-aunt, if she was still with us, would skin me alive if I allowed you to put yourself in danger. Honestly, I don't see another way to bring them to justice, but I can't give you my blessing to continue. As you know, the Van Buren fortune to which you are heir presumptive is not inconsiderable...'

I register the legal phrase. 'Heir presumptive' means if I don't die.

'But to go up against the Parslows, the Jorqueras, the Arblasters and the Winslows, not to mention Lewis Walpole and his fortune and influence, you're going to need something even more substantial than the Van Buren word. You're going to need recorded evidence.'

'Which was the whole point of the plan.'

He leans forward too and clasps his hands together on the desk, as if in prayer. 'Brat,' he says. 'Give it up. Take the money. Now that your Great-Aunt Bunny – God rest her soul – is dead, if something happens to you the school will get the bequest from your great-uncle. You really want that? You want to enrich The Gloomth? Why not live a quiet life, take the inheritance? You'd be going to college next summer anyway. Go to a nice Ivy

League, or somewhere sunny on the west coast. Stanford, Caltech. Put all this behind you, move on.'

'I can't,' I say, much more loudly than I'd meant. 'Don't you see? I *can't* have a quiet life, knowing that they have got away with this. Ulysses Parslow tried to *kill* me. He thought he'd succeeded. That's why he doesn't believe I am really me. And if I don't stop them,' I add, thinking of Jess, 'they'll do this again, to someone else.'

'But they are leaving New Haven too,' Seamark says evenly.

'Their successors then. This thing is passed down the generations. You were in The Gloomth. *You* know.'

'Yes,' he says. 'I do know.'

'Have *you* had a quiet life? Have *you* moved on? Do *you* want them to get away with it?'

'No,' he says, dropping his gaze to his clasped hands. 'No, I don't. I'm a seventy-two-year-old man, and I still wake at night crying about what Lewis Walpole did to me. He was in my year, and I was one of the first Squabs when he founded The Gloomth. He was my Ulysses Parslow.'

Then he looks at me and I see the exact same expression as when I look in the mirror, the expression of someone who has seen things he can't forget.

'All right then,' I say. 'So I'm going ahead tomorrow. For you, for me, for Jess, for every boy who still can't sleep at night.'

He leans across the desk and shakes my hand, like we've just done a business deal.

Which, in a way, we have.

On Saturday, the morning of The Gloomth dinner at Strawberry Hill Villa, I know I have one more visit to make.

I put on a hoodie and a baseball cap, and wear sunglasses against the bright New England fall sunlight. Then I set off for Grove End Cemetery. My feet take me there just as they'd done the night of the Squab dinner, and again when I broke into Yale Med. The reason I know the way so well is that I'd been there many times before, always dressed like this. In the year that I was Eddie Dontay, I came here a lot. It was risky, but I felt like I had to come, particularly as, at Bunny's own request, I'd missed her funeral. I hadn't been to her grave since returning to New Haven School, not even when I'd been twice to Theophilus Eaton's nearby tomb. I needed to come, because after today, I may never come back.

I walk under the grand Egyptian Gate where I'd once taken a heart from a jar, and head to the family tomb, which has four stone angels standing sentinel on each corner. Carved letters grooved into the stone, as big as my hand, are black with slices of shadow in the sun.

There are my ancestors, right back to the *Mayflower*, their birth and death dates in increasingly faded script. But the newest of all reads:

BELINDA VAN BUREN
1934–2026

'Hello, Aunt Bunny,' I say.

Now, I know she's not actually here, she's in the morgue at Yale Med, but it doesn't really make a difference. Here I talk to her like I used to. I would squeeze into her favourite chair in the evenings, and feel her arm around me, and never doubt that I was loved. I'd smell her favourite drink, whiskey and ginger, and when I was older she'd even give me a sip. She'd be dressed immaculately, white hair in its customary bun. She'd have slippers on instead of her outdoor court shoes but that was the only concession she would make to comfort. I never saw her in so much as a dressing gown or a robe – she wouldn't be seen dead in such a thing. Except I had seen her dead. Possibly the cruellest thing The Gloomth had done to me, crueller than the grave. Here at the family tomb, where I will one day lie, I can remember her properly, not a bag of papery flesh on a slab.

Aunt Bunny was the nearest thing I'd had to a mother. My parents were gone, in a car accident – that filmic cliché that Hollywood writers use when they want to get a couple of parents cleanly out of the way so that the rest of the plot can happen. But that was my reality. I'd been too little to really know Great-Uncle Jebediah before he died, so Bunny had been everything to me. She wasn't a cosy woman – she had corners and angles and elbows. She wasn't a cuddler, but I'd never been in any doubt about how much I was loved. She wasn't one for fairytales either, but every night she'd read to me from something infinitely better: classic novels. And my very favourite of all had been *The Count of Monte Cristo*. It had everything: adventure, romance, revenge.

'And the best damned piece of advice a man could ever get,' she'd say. 'That all human wisdom is contained in these two words: Wait and Hope.'

'You were right about that, Aunt Bunny,' I say. And today I'm going to tell her about all the waiting and hoping I'd been doing over the last year.

I'd begun my term at New Haven excited by a new school, new year and new friends. Encouraged by Aunt Bunny, I'd signed up to pledge for The Gloomth, the society which had been so important to Uncle Jebediah that he'd left all his money to the society in the event of the passing of his heirs. My determination was sharpened by the fact that the young heir to the rival Parslow family, Ulysses, was pledging too.

I'd invited Harper to the Feathers Ball. She had impressed me not just with her beauty but with her seeming antipathy to Ulysses. We'd made a connection, kissed and I'd even revealed some of the forbidden secrets of my pledges so far. Then we'd agreed to meet at midnight at New Year, in front of *Hero and Leander*, my favourite picture in Yale Art Gallery.

But I was destined never to make it there. I'd made it through all the pledges, each one darker than the last, until Lewis Walpole had taught us a story I knew I would never be able to read again.

*The Premature Burial* by Edgar Allan Poe.

A story which ends with the protagonist being buried alive. And that's exactly what I was, and exactly where I would still be if a late-night dog walker hadn't heard the sound of tapping coming from far below the earth. Then refusing to go to the cops but begging to be taken to Seamark's. Turning up there like a mud-covered zombie, tapping on the window, Theodore Seamark working late and dropping his pen in horror at the sight of me. I'd gone there first, instead of the school, because I didn't know if New Haven was safe. I couldn't reveal to anyone that I was still alive. We had to find the dog walker, pay him off with a handsome reward for his silence. On my orders Seamark had the coffin reburied and the ground made good. Then he told the press that the heir to the Van Burens had gone abroad to travel before college.

'And then you came to Seamark's,' I say to Bunny, 'on the pretext of an appointment with your family lawyer. You met me again in the back room. Can you remember how hard you hugged me?' My voice wavers. 'We had to meet there from then on. And then you got ill. And finally I had to be smuggled into Yale Hospital to say goodbye. And do you remember making me promise to get revenge, just like the Count of Monte Cristo? To take down Ulysses Parslow, and the family you hated with him, for doing this to your boy. And making me promise not to come to your funeral, because it would give the whole thing away?' The tears were flowing now. 'A deathbed promise, Aunt Bunny. That's not something a fellow forgets.'

Then I tell her the things she wouldn't have known, couldn't have known. The many, many nights talking to Seamark, a Gloomth alum himself, about how to catch The Gloomth with actual evidence. I'd toyed with the idea of recruiting someone else to infiltrate the society, but I couldn't put them in that sort of danger, couldn't put anyone through what I'd been through. The friends I'd thought I'd made at school, good fellows from solid families – Iggy, Oliver and Lowell – were all accessories to my murder. Then I thought of the one friend I'd made on my own, the one person who had seemed immune to the charms of Ulysses Parslow, and the one friend who worked for a newspaper, albeit a student one.

So I'd grown my hair to cover the fading scar from a coffin's lid, and bleached it, and acquired my surfer tan. Seamark had got me a job at the Ida Barney Commencement Dinner. It was a test, really – I'd only met Harper a few times, but we'd gotten close, and if I could convince her I wasn't Brat, then my whole plan might work. I knew she was a keen journalist, she was down on Ulysses and she would help me investigate the society she was dying to know about. I'd let Harper train me, tell me all the things I already knew, read the books I'd already read, seen the photos of family faces as familiar as my own. And at last I'd returned to New Haven, to that strange reception in literature class. When the Gothic Boys had reacted like they had seen a ghost.

Because, of course, they had. I knew what Harper didn't. That Ulysses Parslow had been so shocked by my reappearance because he *knew* I was dead. And he knew that because he'd killed me. I'd been buried alive and left to die. And so to the little scene in the boathouse. He'd told me he knew that I wasn't Brat, but not why.

But still, he couldn't be easy in his mind. I don't think he could subscribe to Lewis Walpole's theory that I'd really risen from the dead, like Mary Shelley's monster. But he was on his guard. Why would a lookalike turn up at his door? Attempting to take the very same pledge that had killed his double? I think that's when Ulysses knew he'd been rumbled. He needed to get rid of me, whoever I was. It was what happened next that interested me. He did not go to ground, he didn't disband The Gloomth or lie low. His arrogance and entitlement was such that he just pledged the imposter as normal, not changing a thing.

Except one. This year, unlike last, the elimination element to the pledge allowed for just one of us to make it, if the others weren't cut out for The Gloomth. Jess and Calvin were removed from the process, leaving me, the cuckoo in the nest. There could only be one reason. Because they were going to kill me. Again.

Things hadn't entirely gone my way though. I hadn't realised, until I was committed to the scheme, that Harper had known Ulysses so well. Until I'd heard the story of their kiss on the ice, and the engagement, I hadn't fully realised the depth of their love–hate relationship. I don't think I was wrong about what I'd seen at the Feathers Ball. What I'd witnessed on the dance floor when he'd cut in was them rekindling an old romance. Ulysses couldn't bear anyone else having what was supposed to be his. If he couldn't give Harper up to a Van Buren he certainly wasn't going to give her up to some imposter. And now Harper was conflicted too. Now she knew I was the real Brat, she had realised that this boy to whom she was so connected, for better or worse, was a murderer.

I raise my chin. All these spider's webs, of who knows what and who loves who. They don't amount to a hill of beans. I have only one thought in my mind, a driving force, a dark passion that I share with my alias Edmond Dantès.

'Revenge,' I say to Bunny. 'I'm going to get my revenge. If it's the last thing I do. And it might just be.'

As I leave, it seems like a shadow covers the grass. I look up, but there is not a cloud in the searing blue sky. There's no shade.

The graveyard is black with pigeons.

By a quarter to five it's already getting dark and I'm in the dormitory, fully dressed in my Gloomth uniform.

Almost.

The little silver pigeon skull still rests on my nightstand. The camera has been charging all day. I disconnect it and lift it to my face. The green pinprick of light shines in the hollow eye socket like hope.

I look around the dormitory. I'm alone. Of course I'm alone. I speak into the camera.

'Anna,' I say. 'I need you. I know you have no reason to trust me, but I need you to. Don't tell Harper, or the others. Just watch the feed and keep the footage. My life is in danger.'

I stare at the little green light. I don't know what I expected – three flashes for yes, two for no? There's no knowing if Anna has heard me. It's after class; school's out for the day. But the light stays steady – all I can hope for.

I could stop. I could do what Seamark recommended – take my great-uncle's fortune, live in his house, go to college, live an easy life. A pigeon lands on the windowsill with a flurry and a flutter, making me jump.

'Hi,' I say. 'What do *you* think I should do?' He cocks his little head at me, but he has no answer to give. I check the green light. It is still on. I turn back to the window. The pigeon has gone. I pin the skull to my cravat, beak to the left, and head downstairs to the waiting car.

As I walk down the driveway it is thick with pigeons. I'd seen ten this morning, a hundred in the graveyard. Now there must be a thousand, as if the driveway has been scattered with seed. In the graveyard I had found it sinister. Now, having met the pigeon on my windowsill, I find it comforting. I pick my way carefully through these feathered allies, carefully placing my feet, and have the oddest feeling that they are all the Squabs of The Gloomth, stretching back for decades, willing me on in my crusade. For an odd moment I feel like it is no longer just my revenge, but ours.

My second glimpse of Strawberry Hill Villa is much, much scarier than the first. I remember a year ago on this journey, seeing the house for the first time. As before, we all have our own cars, so at least I am spared the social necessity of small talk. With its white wedding-cake walls, fairytale spires and arched windows it could be the Disneyland of New England, but for the fact that I know what lies within those white walls, and it is death. I remember *Moby Dick*, another Gothic novel, and the author saying that the colour white was scarier than the colour black. Tonight I agree. I'm Captain Ahab, and this house is my white whale.

The obligatory torches burn in the driveway, lighting our way. Nothing so modern as floodlights would be permitted to dilute the Gothic atmosphere. The pigeons are here too, this time in their thousands. I'm dropped at the grand entrance and my host, Lewis Walpole, is there to greet me, dressed as I have only seen him once before. His silhouette, backed by the blazing lights of the house, could be a figure from fable, with a cane and frockcoat. As I follow him into the atrium I can see his garb clearly. Below the portrait of his famous ancestor he turns so I can fully appreciate the outlandishness of his outfit. He is wearing a powdered periwig over his own white hair, a long waistcoat of figured orange silk and a jacket of crushed teal velvet. He is wearing exactly the same as the man in the painting, right down to the creamy frilled shirt and snowy cravat. Tonight, as last year, he is cosplaying as the original Gothic writer, author of *The Castle of Otranto* and inventor of the word *Gloomth*, Horace Walpole.

The professor throws out his arms. 'Welcome!' he booms. I'm not too sure what to do – whether I'm supposed to throw myself on his bosom. So I just wait.

The atrium is a circle, and from four connecting doors the four members of The Gloomth appear, like characters in a melodrama. They are all immaculate in their uniforms, their pigeon skulls facing to the right. Ulysses strolls up to me like a catwalk model. He shakes my hand and claps me on the shoulder.

'Good to see you again, old man,' he says. It's an odd intonation, as if he hasn't seen me for a year, rather than at breakfast this morning. The sense of foreboding, which was just a seed in the car, blooms and blossoms into a black flower.

Lewis Walpole's cane taps on the marble floors as he leads us from one magnificent room to the next, all carefully curated over the centuries by the various generations of the Committee of Taste. I follow obediently. I remember the tour from last year, the memories etched on my mind with a sharp point. I remember above all the colours – in contrast to the white exterior of the house there is no absence of colour inside. One great drawing room is a vivid blue, leading to a parlour painted purple, then a morning room painted green, an orange ballroom and a white chapel. My knees start to shake. I remember, because there is no shutting off the maze-like pathways of my mind now, that according to Poe in *The Masque of the Red Death*, all of these colours corresponded to the ages of man. Blue for birth, purple for youth and green for adolescence. Orange represented adulthood, white stood for old age, violet denoted imminent death and black signalled death itself. So as we emerge from the white and silver chapel, I know what's coming next.

'Now, gentlemen,' says Lewis Walpole, holding out his arms expansively once again. 'Let us dine.'

We follow him to the dining room. And the unescapable feature of the great hall, which hits you right behind the eyeballs as soon as you enter the space, is that it is painted a vivid violet.

The colour of imminent death.

We sit at table, in places designated by a pigeon feather painted with our names in gold letters. There is also a menu resting on each plate, listing the bill of fare at this most Gothic of feasts. It reads:

### Appetisers:
Delectable sandwiches with unknown fillings
and a mysterious flavour – *Rebecca*,
Daphne du Maurier (1938)

### Main courses:
Paprika Hendl (traditional Hungarian stew) – *Dracula*,
Bram Stoker (1897)
Savoury bread pudding 'with layers of bread, mustardy custard, and wine-caramelized onions' – *Frankenstein*,
Mary Shelley (1818)
Pheasant with hazelnuts and chocolate – *The Bloody Chamber*,
Angela Carter (1979)

### Dessert:

'Great cake' – *Great Expectations*, Charles Dickens (1861)
'Yolk-yellow sponge dotted with caraway seeds' – *Jane Eyre*,
Charlotte Brönte (1847)
Peach shortcakes – *The Haunting of Hill House*,
Shirley Jackson (1959)

So all the foods are from Gothic novels. Neat. I'd be delighted by the ingenuity if this was some school ball or Halloween party. And some of the foods featured are among my favourites. But tonight that's no comfort. It feels more like those gladiators of old who got a slap-up dinner before meeting the lions, or prisoners on death row, who ask for their favourite final meal.

Far from hungry, I nibble at the tiny sandwiches that serve as appetisers with our aperitifs. We raise our glasses with the traditional Gloomth toast: *Even in the Grave All is Not Lost*, and of course the words have an extra resonance for me. Lewis Walpole is clearly perfectly happy to serve alcohol to underage kids, but I suppose when you've broken pretty much every commandment a little thing like federal law doesn't bother you. I can feel eyes on me, looking at me expectantly. I get an eerie feeling that as well as being the condemned man I am the guest of honour, and everyone is looking to me for entertainment.

'Did you know,' I say as an opening gambit, 'that the most requested death row food is McDonald's?'

'I believe that,' says Iggy, someone who I am fairly sure has never seen the inside of a McDonald's.

'Why?' I ask, interested.

'Because of the socio-economic demographic of most criminals.'

I look around the table at all of the Gothic Boys, these sons of senators and Supreme Court judges and Spanish princes, and the eminent multimillionaire professor dressed as his noble ancestor Horace Walpole, Earl of Oxford and member of the British parliament. The cream of high society, and all murderers.

'You really think criminality is a poor man's game?' I let my scepticism sound in my voice.

'Well, of course,' says Lowell. 'They don't know any better.'

I used to be like them. Until I was Eddie Dontay for a year and walked in the shoes of the minimum-wage stiff, working for the man and living in a scummy walk-up on the wrong side of town. Now I know what it's like to wash dishes until my fingertips wrinkle, to be so tired I can hardly see, to spend my days taking food orders from rich assholes like them, to go home smelling of burger grease and coffee grounds and exhaustion. At the time, it sucked, and the only thing that kept me going was the bitter diesel of revenge. But now I'm glad I did it. If I die tonight, I die a better man than I was.

'You know,' I say aloud, thinking of Stacey, who kept me alive at Marty's Café, and Anna, the Ida Barney scholarship girl, 'some of the best people I know don't have a dime. So I highly doubt if everyone on death row is on welfare.'

Iggy ignores the social commentary and steers us back to the original subject. 'What would you have as your last meal?'

'Sushi,' I say without hesitation. 'Although I can never understand how condemned men can manage to tuck into their favourite foods the night before they die.' Personally, I have no appetite at all. I know that at some point tonight I will once again be fighting for my life. I don't know exactly how, but I know it will have something to do with a pendulum.

And a pit.

'Perhaps it is something to do with necessity,' says Lewis Walpole in a considered fashion. 'Although I am sure death row inmates are tolerably well fed, the gladiators of old who were granted *cena libera*, or free meal, before they died, were almost starved. Like your hero Edmond Dantès, the Count of Monte Cristo, who was on starvation rations for fourteen years in prison. In the novel you *insisted* was Gothic.' He sounds amused.

'Oh, it definitely is Gothic,' I say. 'No question.' I have nothing to lose, no shits left to give. What are they going to do, kill me? I already know that's what they have planned. There's a kind of confidence that comes with certainty.

'Perhaps you will humour us with your thesis,' says Lewis Walpole as silent servants bring round the pheasant. 'One final time. Why are you so adamant that *The Count of Monte Cristo* is a Gothic novel?'

*One final time.* At least he's not even bothering to pretend I'll live beyond tonight, and I kind of appreciate his honesty. I have to get a confession on camera. Yes, I want above all to take Ulysses down, but I want to take Walpole down with him. Otherwise he can carry on doing this, bolstered by wealth and respectability and heritage, forever. Plus, I promised Seamark I'd do this; the elderly lawyer was still a terrified schoolboy when I looked in his watery eyes.

'OK,' I say. 'I'll answer you that if you'll answer me another. Am I the first one to come back?'

Lewis Walpole inclines his head. 'Yes. You have the honour of being The Gloomth society's first revenant.'

'What's a revenant?' I ask.

'One who rises from the dead,' the professor replies. 'The root of the word is the French noun *revenir*, literally "to return".'

I know why he's speaking with such freedom. It's because he is confident I will not survive the night. He's like one of those supervillains who is happy to explain, in great detail, the mechanism of a trap to his victim. Once you're inside.

'Why do this?' I ask. 'You could be a philanthropist instead.'

'I believe that I *am* a philanthropist,' he says, 'in the truest sense. I make boys feel alive, like never before. When you stare death in the face, that is when you most love life. Or, to quote from your favourite novel: "It is necessary to have wished for death in order to know how good it is to have lived". You think Jess will ever forget the moment the dark water of the lake entered his lungs? Will Calvin ever forget almost choking on verdant vomit, the hue of the Green Fairy? We are moulding America's future. *This* is how you make men.'

'It's not how you make men,' I say, thinking of Seamark. 'It's how you make frightened little boys. And sometimes things go awry, don't they? How many have you killed over the years?'

Lewis Walpole shrugs. It's the most callous gesture I've ever seen in my life, the indifference somehow crueller than any of his other many sins. 'Tens perhaps. Not hundreds. But again, we are shaping America. This is the survival of the fittest. Like you. Can you really deny the fact that you have become who you really are in this last year? We did you a favour.'

He's right. I can't deny it. But I can't say I would have chosen this path.

'Now, come. Quid pro quo,' he probes. 'Why is *The Count of Monte Cristo* a Gothic novel, in your view?'

I take a swallow of wine – my throat is suddenly dry. These are all the finest vintages, but this one tastes a little bitter, and gritty. 'Well,' I begin. 'The whole novel is about revenge. That could hardly be more Gothic. Edmond Dantès is framed for a crime he didn't commit, and his relentless pursuit of revenge against those who wronged him is a common theme in Gothic literature.' I don't say that's the theme of my story too. 'There's also a mysterious and isolated setting: the dungeons of the prison island of Château d'If, Dantès' home for fourteen years. Then, of course the treasure island of Monte Cristo, to which he escapes to discover his fabulous wealth.' I look about me as I speak. I realise that I am now in the mysterious and isolated setting myself, the place where the final act of my own Gothic drama will play out. Strawberry Hill Villa is fabulously wealthy; also a prison. 'The count is a brooding and vengeful protagonist, a common Gothic archetype. He is also a romantic hero, a renegade who rejects society.' Just as I had done for a whole year, when I hid myself away as Eddie Dontay. 'There's a damsel in distress, Mercedes, who was his childhood sweetheart, lost to the very man who wronged him. There's even' – I look directly at Lewis Walpole – 'a secret society called the Carbonari. That's another staple of the Gothic novel. But who knows that better than you?'

He looks at me, stroking his beard. Just as he did a year ago in class, when I first said all this to him. 'Interesting,' he says.

For the following courses, the Paprika Hendl and the pheasant with hazelnuts, The Gloomth discuss the novel, for all the world as if this was some sort of literary salon, not a condemned man's last meal. What did Lewis Walpole call it? A *cena libera*. Everyone joins in, everyone has something to say. Except Ulysses Parslow, who sits watching from his silver eyes. Then at last, he speaks for the first time. Such is his power that everyone hushes around him, even his host.

'There's one element of your theory on which I must take issue with you. The damsel in distress. Mercedes was never in distress. She chose her fate.'

He takes something sleek and shiny from his pocket and holds it up to my face. At first I think it's a mirror. Then I see it is a phone.

My old phone.

I haven't seen it for a year, since it was the difference between life and death for me. And of course, confronted by my features, the face ID automatically unlocks it. I might have fooled Harper, and maybe Ulysses, but there is no fooling biometrics. And there, on the lock screen, is a selfie of Harper and me together. I took it at the Feathers Ball last year.

I go to take the phone. But Ulysses does that thing that you might do with a child – he moves it out of my reach and holds it high.

'You see,' he says. 'You made a fundamental misunderstanding. When you said Harper was Mercedes, you were right. She is indeed the childhood sweetheart of the hero. She was, briefly, lost to another. But then she reunited with her true love. And *I* am the hero of the story, not you.'

I look at Harper's face on the lockscreen, her shining, beautiful, innocent face. But now I see her with new eyes.

There's no way Ulysses could have known that I called Harper 'Mercedes' at the Feathers Ball.

No way, that is, unless she told him.

'Yes,' says Ulysses. 'Now you understand. Harper was never in distress either. We are back together. She's not coming to save you.' As I stare, with betrayal, accusation, realisation, Harper's features seem to shimmer and move around, until she looks like a Picasso. My blood sings in my ears, sweat prickles on my lip.

*The bitterness in the wine.*

Then her whole picture blurs, and I slip from consciousness.

# 9

I wake but I can't move. I am strapped to some sort of frame, looking at a portrait on a far wall. It seems to be a portrait of Father Time. As my eyes focus, I realise that Father Time is Lewis Walpole – it's a portrait of him, white beard and all.

Then, as I regain full consciousness, the weight of my flesh and muscle tells me I am actually on my back, which means that the picture is way above my head and attached directly to the ceiling. I try to move my head – I can turn it enough to see that I am in a dim circular room, just like in Poe's story. The only light source seems to be emanating from the picture, and nameless creatures skitter in the shadows on little scrabbling claws.

It's unsettling being under the gaze of the picture. I stare back at Father Time and it seems to me that, in the best haunted house tradition, the eyes move.

Someone is observing me from behind the picture.

There is a slicing, sliding sound and suddenly the canvas slides open. It reveals not the aged face of Lewis Walpole, but, like Dorian Gray's picture, the youthful beauty of Ulysses Parslow.

'Hello, Brat,' he says.

My eyes must have widened, my pupils must have dilated, my muscles must have given an involuntary jerk.

'Yes,' he says. 'Now *you're* afraid of *me*.'

I can't deny it. I can't say anything.

'You know, when I first saw you in back in class this year, I was afraid of you. You saw it, didn't you? I really did think you were a lookalike, that someone knew what we'd done, and you'd come to take us down. When you started telling us about Dubai and Madagascar and Thailand, all the places the postcards had come from, we really started to worry.'

'You sent the postcards to yourselves, I suppose?' I ask.

'Of course,' he says. 'It was easy. We bought the cards online, and Oliver does a passable imitation of your handwriting. Only Lewis Walpole was delighted when you turned up. He thought you really had come back from the dead. He thought we'd called forth some dark forces and that you had risen from the grave to take your revenge. Then Harper told me about your little ruse, the aliases you'd used, the names from *The Count of Monte Cristo*. So once she came clean, we went to dig up the coffin where you'd lain.'

'The coffin where *you'd* left me.' I have to get him to admit it on camera.

'If you prefer. Anyway, you weren't there. You were working in that shabby little diner.'

Of all the things to get offended about at this moment, I bristle at his dismissal of Marty's.

'You see, I know all about you, Brat. Something else I know about you: this year you came prepared. You were hoping to catch us this time, weren't you? There was something you carried with you at all times. Something at your throat. Something to record your whereabouts.'

I can't, of course, put my hand to my throat. But I lower my chin to my chest in a panic. It's all right. The pigeon skull is still there. But has Harper told him about the camera? Did she know I'd been lying when I said it had been wrecked in the lake? Is that what he's talking about? Then Ulysses dangles something from the hatch. Something golden and sparkling.

'Your Van Buren medallion. We found the GPS tracker inside the locket. You thought you'd been very clever, didn't you?'

'Clearly not as clever as you.' I fight to keep the triumph out of my voice. Let him think he's won this one, really incriminate himself.

'You know,' he says, as if to himself, 'I think I will keep this medallion. Not as a trophy though. Nothing so trivial. I'm keeping it because we can't have anyone knowing you died here. You have to die abroad, and this pendant will help us identify some poor stranger as you. A tragic fire, I think, in a Bangkok hotel room, or a drowning in Madagascar, perhaps. Somewhere we wrote the postcards from. Burned to a crisp, bloated by the tide beyond recognition.' His enjoyment of the prospect of what his all-powerful society will do to some stranger is hideously Gothic. 'We'll make it impossible to identify the body. Except for this.' He holds up the little winking medallion.

'And when I'm gone, what then?' I say, drawing him out. 'Your society is finished. You haven't replaced your number.'

'Not a bit of it,' says Ulysses smoothly. 'We fully intend to pledge next term. There's nothing in our rules that states that we have to pledge only in the fall. We just needed to wait until you were dead.'

This is good stuff. I can only pray that Anna is recording this, and then even if I don't make it through the night, she'll have the footage. 'Seamark knows where I am,' I say with perfect truth.

'Seamark told the press you were travelling,' says Ulysses. This is also true – he did it on my instructions. 'Once your body is recovered you think anyone will believe the paranoid ramblings of a senile lawyer?'

'He's Walpole's age,' I say. If he's going to take down my guy I'm going to take down his. 'They were in The Gloomth together. If Seamark is senile, so is your pet professor.'

'Oh, Walpole's definitely insane, no question. That's what makes him such delicious company.' He sighs happily. 'It was he who designed *the* most perfect way to get rid of you. Of course, it would be so much easier if you drove. Car crashes are much easier to orchestrate. According to Professor Walpole anyway.'

My God. My *God*. Is he actually saying what I think he's saying? 'My parents,' I choke. I can barely get the words out. 'Was that . . . was that The Gloomth too?' The car crash, fifteen years ago. The reason they have never been any more to me than a photograph on Bunny's bedside table and a vague memory of my mother's favourite song – 'Blackbird' by the Beatles.

'Of course Lewis was responsible,' he says, as if explaining something to a child. 'Your great-uncle couldn't have any surviving male heirs if The Gloomth was to inherit his fortune.'

Tears leak from my eyes, just as they had the night I'd lain next to Bunny.

'Christ,' I whisper. 'Christ!' I shout. 'What made you this way? Was it what happened to Timmie? Did her accident twist you into this . . . this pretzel of evil?'

He smiles down at me like a benevolent deity. 'Bless you, Brat. *I* killed Timmie.'

I lie still, letting this new horror sink in.

'Think about it,' he says. 'I had been an only child for six years. I was the sun in my parents' universe. Then *she* came along.' There is venom in the voice. 'And my time in the sun was over. They doted on her. I lived in the shadow, watching. So that day on the ice, when Harper took her brother back to the house, I pushed her through the ice, and I held her down so she couldn't get out. Then I walked back to meet Harper, in time for our first kiss.'

I begin to make some unearthly noise, half gasp and half hiccup. It's as if I am trying to drink in the horror of it, but the horror keeps coming, pouring down from his lips, waterboarding me until I'm drowning in it. How could someone drown his sister, and then seconds later enjoy his first kiss?

'You see,' he continues. 'I will never, Brat, let anyone take what's mine. You should know that by now.'

He's talking about Harper. 'If Harper ever finds out . . .'

'She won't,' he says. 'But she *gets* me. "He was persuaded he could know no happiness but in the society of one with whom he could forever indulge the melancholy that had taken possession of his soul."' I recognise the quote. Of course I do. It's from *The Castle of Otranto*, the book that started it all.

And now we have come to an ending.

'Well, Brat,' Ulysses calls from far above. 'I must be going.

Lewis has rather a nice little dessert wine that I've been longing to try. I *think* it has been nice knowing you.'

He retreats, but before I can feel the relief of his absence something is lowered through the hatch with the clunk of a pulley and the singing of a blade. Something I've been expecting all evening.

A pendulum.

## 10

This is new.

Last year when I entered the Premature Burial pledge, there was nothing quite so elaborate – no circular room, no pendulum, just the bitter, gritty wine and the realisation that I was in a box buried somewhere in the godforsaken undergrowth. This year they have been far more cunning. This year I can *see* my own approaching death, the razor-sharp pendulum, a foot long from horn to horn, descending little by little until it will be low enough to slice, first through my Gloomth uniform, and then through my flesh, spilling my guts like groceries.

I panic. Of course I do. I yank at my bonds, threshing and twisting, gasping as if I'm running, wearing myself out until I start to feel light-headed. And still the shining blade descends, inch by inch, like a terrible pendulum on some celestial grandfather clock. For the second time in my short life, I know exactly the moment that I'm going to die.

My mind detonates into a million splintered, nonsensical thoughts, uppermost of which is the regret that I never got to take Anna Sato to Marty's. I see us, in my final movie montage, laughing together over a cup of Stacey's legendary coffee. I must be delirious. This is no good.

I force myself to lie perfectly still and *think*. I feel around my bonds, trying to find some sort of release. My fingers meet something soft and slimy, and a bloody, butcher's smell rises to my nose. I remember the story from class – *meat left for the prisoner, smeared across his bonds to attract . . . the rats.* I grab at the flesh and smear it around my bonds as best I can. Something runs across my chest and I cry out – the pride leaves my body with the scream. I force myself to lie as still as I can while one, then two, then a dozen gnawing mouths bite at the ropes that bind me – I can't afford to scare them away. Even when their sharp little teeth fasten on to the bloody flesh of my wrists and ankles, I try not to flinch.

The pendulum is so close now that I can feel the disturbance of the air as it swishes past my face, parting my hair. One foot is loose, and I kick away the ropes. Then one hand comes free and I use it to free the other one, judiciously timing my efforts to avoid the lowering blade. In the nick of time, I roll off the frame, just as the blade clashes into the wood, smashing through the centre. I sit with my back to the wall, breathing heavily, watching. The pendulum retracts, taking the frame with it, through the hatch in the ceiling. Now there is nothing in the room but me and my saviours the rats, who gather boldly at my wrists and ankles to lick up the vestiges of blood, and have to be swiped away.

Now the frame is gone I can see what was beneath me all along. A dark pit, so black I can't see the depth of it, even when I crawl gingerly to the lip. It seems as dark as a tear in the universe itself, the veil between our world and a netherworld of nameless horror. Great evil emanates from it, an audible hiss of a thousand whispers, and I back away as far as I can go, right until my back is pressed against the circular wall. I'm sweating with the terror and effort of my escape, my back burning. Then I realise that the heat isn't coming from me.

It is coming from the wall.

The black turns to ash grey, then orange, then bright red, just like a stove heating up. I have to move away from the wall before it parts me from my flesh. Only on the very edge of the pit can I find some relief. And then, just like in the story, the walls begin to move in towards me, the circle contracting, growing smaller and smaller, the floor disappearing.

Then I realise. The frame was *designed* so I would escape the pendulum. That was part of the game. They *wanted* me to end up in the pit. This is the part where Toledo falls, the trumpets sound and a hand pulls me to freedom. But nothing happens; no liberating armies, no blaring bugles, no helping hand. Forced to choose between the pit and the fire I do the only thing I can.

I jump.

I fall and fall, six feet, twelve, eighteen, infinity. At last I hit a surface and crumple into a confined space, my arms and legs flex and my limbs hit the sides and bottom of a box. I have returned to my nightmare. Far above me, as if I am at the bottom of the well, I can see a disc of the red of the room like a sickly sun. I try to get up, but a heavy lid closes, striking me on the head. I black out.

# 11

'Ulysses?'

'Brat?' The voice of his friend is a huge comfort for him.

'Where are we?'

'In a box, I think.'

The two friends lie close, side by side, arms pinned to their sides. There is only space for one, but there are two of them down there.

'I have my phone,' says Brat. 'But I can't move my hand.'

'Wait,' says Ulysses. 'I'll get it.'

He fumbles in Brat's pocket for the phone, and with difficulty in the confined space, holds it up to Brat's face. The dim light is enough to illuminate Brat's features, which unlock the phone. There is the selfie of Brat and Harper, a couple of weeks ago at the Feathers Ball. The thought that he might never see her again makes Brat want to cry. Ulysses sees the tears but not the reason.

'Don't worry,' he says. 'This is all part of it. They wouldn't let us die.'

Now the phone is activated, Ulysses is able to click on the torch, and as the light sweeps around the small space, they realise just how dire their situation is.

'This is not just a box,' says Brat, his voice unsteady. 'It's a coffin. And there's only room for one.'

'We'll just kick our way out,' says Ulysses.

'But what if we are buried?' Brat says. 'Under six feet of earth?' His breathing is becoming faster.

'Don't panic,' says Ulysses. 'It uses up oxygen.' He knocks on the coffin lid – there is a hollow booming sound, not the dead sound of six feet of earth. 'Nothing above us,' he says. 'Come on. On my count, push your knees as hard as you can against the lid.'

Brat trusts him. After all, they've been best friends all term. They think the same, they know all the same people, they laugh at the same jokes, they get the same literary references. They never thought they would be friends, but they are. They could double-handedly end the age-old Parslow/Van Buren feud and coexist side by side, just like the houses of the Van Buren family crest, just like they lie now in this box.

On the count of three, working together as a team, they both kick out. The lid starts to bounce open and slam shut again, but on the third heave the lid flips back. They are in a grave, six-feet deep; and the moon shines above, offering redemption like a communion wafer.

Ulysses clambers out first. He stands above Brat, a foot on either of the coffin's sides. In one hand he holds Brat's phone. Brat holds a hand up to him to haul him out. For a moment Ulysses looks at the hand – dirty and elemental, reaching up from the earth. Then he looks Brat in the eyes, with his direct silver gaze.

'You were right,' he says. 'There is only room for one.'

Then he slams the lid down hard.

Brat kicks again, but now there's only one of him, and Ulysses is standing on the lid of the coffin. He screams and punches out, *desperate, until his knuckles are raw. Then all at once he stops fighting.*

*Bartholomew Van Buren III knows exactly the moment that he's going to die.*

*Forcing himself to stay calm, he assesses the situation:*

*He is trapped underground, in a seven-foot by two-foot coffin, the air stifling, the oxygen rapidly running out. Added to that, his mortal enemy is standing on the lid, so he cannot escape.*

*But even now, that indomitable little flame called Hope burns stubbornly and will not be extinguished. Surely this is part of the pledge? Surely his enemy will relent, open the lid and pull him to freedom? Surely they will all laugh about this later, about how scared he had been?*

*But then he hears the voice he knows as well as his own, from six feet above. And the sound that tells him it is over:*

*The brutal death rattle of earth hitting the coffin lid, like dark hail.*

## 12

I awake from my nightmare of a year ago, to the terrible realisation that once again I am in a coffin. So life, or rather death, has come full circle.

This time I am alone. There is no Ulysses Parslow jammed next to me. Someone I thought was a friend, but actually turned out to be my murderer.

I try to regulate my breathing, stem the rising tide of panic, conscious of what Ulysses said about conserving oxygen.

I kick out, just like we did together, trying to use my knees as leverage. But there's only one of me. I knock on the coffin lid, just as Ulysses did last year, and this time there is no hollow boom, but the smothered dead sound of six feet of earth. Either they've moved me to a burial ground, or they've filled in the pit with earth.

This year I don't even have my phone. Ulysses still has it. So my only one, tiny hope, the one pinprick of light, is the tiny emerald glow of the camera, which gives this two foot by six foot space a glow of green. Rather than looking eerie, the hue is comforting. It means that, actually, I'm *not* alone. It means that Anna is with me.

Or is she? It must be the small hours of the morning by now. Who would stay up far into the night at a weekend? A girl like that, she's probably out at a party, hooking up with some guy. Somehow that thought is the most miserable of all.

I make a decision. Even if she watches this back in the morning, when I'm long dead, I still want her to know what I want her to know. I raise my hands to my throat and unpin the silver pigeon skull. I turn him around – beak to the right, so his eye is facing me. I take a deep breath – perhaps one of my last, and address Anna directly.

'I don't know if you can hear me,' I say. 'I'm buried in a coffin below Strawberry Hill Villa. In a pit under a circular room, which is probably in the cellar. The GPS will bring you to the house, but I no longer have it, Ulysses does.' I pause. I'm getting breathless – the air is very thin. I can feel myself slipping from consciousness. But that's not even what I really wanted to tell you. I wanted to say . . .' My voice cracks like the rasp of Poe's raven. 'I want you to know that when you kissed me at the Feathers Ball, and I kissed you back, I meant it. I've told a lot of lies but that was the truth.'

I have no more energy, no more air. My grip loosens and the pigeon skull rolls from my hand. I drift in and out of being, conscious only of a raging thirst. My final thought is of The Gloomth toast.

*Even in the Grave All is Not Lost.*

And then a sound, on the coffin lid.

The bite and crunch of a spade biting through earth, the scrape of metal on the lid, clearing earth away. Last year, the sound on the wood had meant death. This year it means life.

The lid lifts – and there is light. Not red now, but blue, the flashing lights of the NHPD. I reach up my hand and, unlike last year, someone takes it and hauls me up. Toledo has fallen, and the sirens sound like trumpets.

I'm being gently lifted and secured to a gurney and rolled through the coloured rooms. Vaguely I register Ulysses, Lewis Walpole and the Gothic Boys being handcuffed and Mirandized. Then I'm in the back of an ambulance and someone is checking the bump on my head. Someone is still holding my hand, and as my vision clears, I see it is Anna Sato. An officer sits opposite with her laptop, my live feed still playing. I fold Anna in my arms. Her silky black hair smells of coconut, of sweetness and sunshine. Her lips find mine, and after the kiss she whispers in my mouth, just as she did at the Feathers Ball.

'I meant it too,' she says. 'I meant it too.'

I hold her tight, face buried in my shoulder, and over her head I see a hundred thousand pigeons rise from the lawn and wheel away into the sky.

# EPILOGUE

On the last day of The Gloomth trial Anna and I go straight from the courthouse to Marty's. I haven't been back since the morning I went to New Haven School, when I left Stacey fifty bucks. But I always knew that straight after the verdict I would take Anna there.

It had been a long trial, and it had attracted a lot of press. It had taken a toll on me too, as I'd had to take the stand for days on end, and give endless depositions and witness statements. But Anna had been with me all the way through. And I'd got what I'd wanted: Ulysses Parslow had been found guilty of murder in the first degree of Ctimene Parslow, and attempted murder of Bartholomew Van Buren III. Ignatio Jorquera, Oliver Arblaster and Lowell Bell-Cross had been found guilty of being accessories to attempted murder. As all the boys were under the age of criminal responsibility they were sent to a juvenile correctional facility. Lewis Walpole was found guilty of multiple counts of actual bodily harm, attempted murder and first-degree murder over the years. He had been imprisoned for life. The DA's office had granted a warrant to pull Strawberry Hill

Villa apart looking for human remains. Multiple other historical charges had been filed going back decades, and many other victims had come forward, their statements coordinated by the eminent lawyer Theodore Seamark, who himself had been a victim of The Gloomth.

The Ida Barney girls, who had been so instrumental in exposing the society, had all had to give evidence, which wasn't great for them. But they could now add the biggest news story to shake American society since Watergate to their college applications. I'd kept Harper's connections to Ulysses Parslow out of the story as much as possible. She'd been guilty of nothing but falling under his spell, and I'd done that myself in that first term of knowing him.

I'd left New Haven – I was done with school, and didn't want to go to an Ivy League, where I suspected the fraternities and societies of New Haven would just be replicated. I now had the Van Buren fortune and never needed to work – I could just be a rich, useless asshole but I didn't want that either. In the end, I'd arranged with Seamark that I would join the firm as a junior clerk. He was going to train me up, I would do an apprenticeship Law degree and I would eventually take over. I had a new-found interest in justice, a much healthier goal than revenge. In the meantime, with the Van Buren fortune I had set up an educational trust for kids on welfare. I wasn't about to let other Lewis Walpoles shape America's young men.

I clink my coffee cup against Anna's. 'To justice,' she says, as if she read my mind.

'Even in the Grave All is Not Lost,' I say in response.

'What?' she says.

'It's the toast of The Gloomth,' I say.

'The now defunct Gloomth.' She smiles. She's smiled a lot since we've been together. And it always makes my heart fail.

I smile back. 'The now defunct Gloomth. I looked up the full quote in *The Castle of Otranto*. It goes: "In death – no! even in the grave all is not lost. Else there is no immortality for man. Arousing from the most profound slumbers, we break the gossamer web of some dream. Yet in a second afterward (so frail may that web have been) we remember not that we have dreamed."'

Anna looks down into her cup. 'Do you think you'll ever forget?'

'No,' I say. 'But that's OK.'

'It is,' she says. 'Remember kintsugi? Something that is broken can be more beautiful than it was before.'

I smile at her. 'Now I need to do something with the life I've been given.'

'We all do,' she says. 'And help others make the most of their lives too.'

'Speaking of which,' I say. Stacey is approaching our table, smile wider than a mile. I get up to greet her. That chivalry bullshit dies hard.

'Sit your behind down,' she says, 'and scootch along.'

I move along the booth to make room.

'You didn't talk to me last time,' she says, wagging her finger in my face. 'Oh, I knew it was you. I just thought you were too snooty to say hello once you had your fancy new clothes and your fancy new haircut and your fancy new girlfriend.' She twinkles across the table at Anna. 'I like this one much better.'

'Me too,' I say, smiling.

'At least you're in the game now.' Stacey looks at me approvingly. 'Learned to get what you want, did ya?'

I shrug. 'As a wise woman once said: "You gotta do what them pigeons do. Shit on everyone else before they shit on you."'

She laughs, then her face grows serious. 'Don't suppose I can get you to come back here? Best busboy I ever had.'

I shake my head. 'Nope, sorry. But you can employ someone else.'

'Management will give me some knucklehead,' she says. 'Ain't up to me.'

'Oh, but it is,' I say.

I reach into the inside pocket of my dove-grey court suit.

Stacey raises a tattooed eyebrow. 'Going to leave fifty dollars again?'

'No,' I say. 'I'm going to go one better than that.'

On to the diner table in front of her, among the coffee cups, I place the deeds to Marty's Café, made out in her name and signed:

*Theodore Jeamark*

Old handwriting habits die hard too, I guess.

I've never seen Stacey lost for words before. Anna and I watch her, smiles growing, as the reality sinks in.

Stacey looks from one of us to the other. 'I *own* this place?' she asks.

'Yes,' I say. I nod to the line at the counter. 'Better get back to it. Those are your profits you're losing.'

She gives me a bone-crushing hug, and a big smacker of a kiss on my cheek. Then she goes back to her customers, dabbing her eyes with her apron.

Anna covers my hands with hers. I can feel the warmth of her approval and it feels great. 'What now?' she asks.

There's someone else I need to tell about the verdict. She's not going to hear me, but it's something I need to do. Or maybe she will hear me? *Even in the Grave All is Not Lost.*

'How about a trip to Grove End Cemetery?' I ask. 'There's someone I want you to meet.'

# ACKNOWLEDGEMENTS

I have lots of thank yous to say to those who pledged to come along with me on this journey and embrace The Gloomth.

A huge thank you to the team at Hachette; to ace editor Katie Levy for her unwavering sense of story, to Laura Pritchard and Hazel Cotton for their work on the copyedit and proofs, and to Antara Bate and the whole marketing team for spreading the Gloomth gospel.

Once again I'm indebted to Samuel Perrett for the wonderful cover design.

I wouldn't be writing any of this without my agent Teresa Chris, not just an agent but a friend.

Thank you to my daughter Ruby for helping me out with the Spanish, and to Sacha for the pigeon shit (he knows what this means!)

I'm grateful to dear friend and Gothic Literature whizz Dr Fiona Snailham for telling me about the Committee of Taste and other Gothic matters.

As always I found some great resources online – the Storynory.com website retold the story of Hero and Leander beautifully and inspired my own retelling.

But, as ever, my greatest inspiration was to be found between the pages of a book. Two books in particular formed the spine of this Gothic skeleton.

Firstly, *The Count of Monte Cristo*. This is my favourite ever classic book, and a wonderful story of revenge. But it's also a great novel of redemption, with the best last line ever; 'All human wisdom can be distilled into two words: Wait, and Hope.'

The second is *Brat Farrar* by Josephine Tey, a wonderful novel from which I borrowed elements of plot, and the protagonist's name.

Strawberry Hill House, Horace Walpole's house on which I based Lewis Walpole's villa, is in Twickenham near Richmond-on-Thames, and well worth a visit if you're ever in the area.

Finally, thank you as ever to Ruby, Conrad and Sacha. We are birds of a feather, and we flock together.

© Sacha Bennett

**M. A. Bennett** was born in Manchester to an English mother and a Venetian father. She was raised in Yorkshire, the home of English Gothic. She loved literature so much she studied it at four different universities (including Oxford and Venice).

She then studied art and worked as a designer, actress and film reviewer. Now she has her dream job of being a writer, and her books have been translated into more than 20 languages. She lives in London with one husband, two children and three cats.

# ALSO FROM M. A. BENNETT

# DON'T MISS

# LOOK OUT FOR

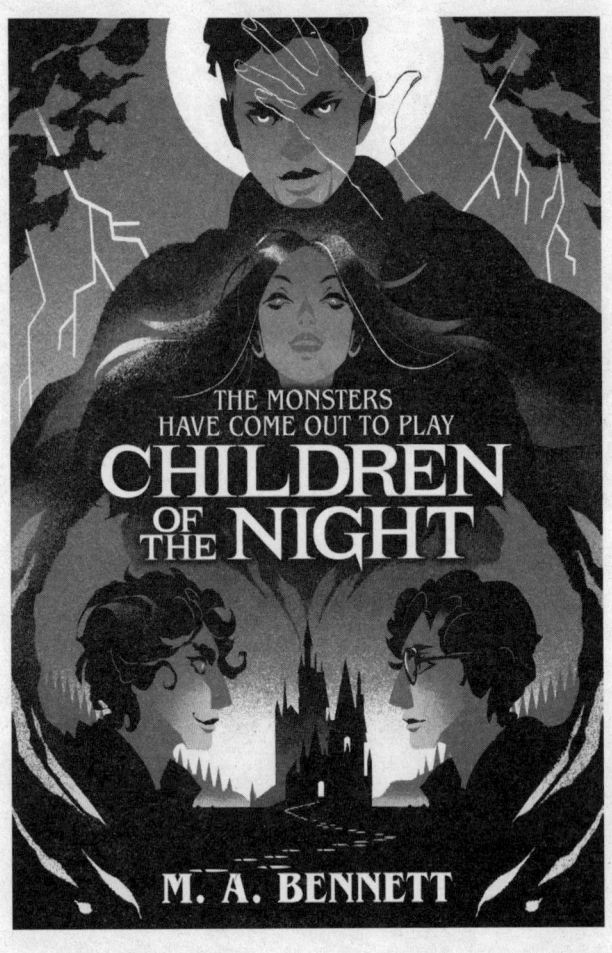